A gift of the
Eunice Gray Fund
of the
Oregon Community Foundation

JACKSON COUNTY
Library Services

THE UNDER DOG
AND OTHER STORIES

Center Point
Large Print

**This Large Print Book carries the
Seal of Approval of N.A.V.H.**

Agatha Christie

THE UNDER DOG
AND OTHER STORIES

A Hercule Poirot Collection

CENTER POINT LARGE PRINT
THORNDIKE, MAINE

This Center Point Large Print edition is published in the year 2014 by arrangement with William Morrow Paperbacks, an imprint of HarperCollins Publishers.

The text of this Large Print edition is unabridged. In other aspects, this book may vary from the original edition. Printed in the United States of America on permanent paper. Set in 16-point Times New Roman type.

ISBN: 978-1-62899-129-1

Library of Congress Cataloging-in-Publication Data

Christie, Agatha, 1890–1976.
[Short stories. Selections]
The Under dog and other stories : a Hercule Poirot collection / Agatha Christie. — Center Point Large Print Edition.
pages cm.
Summary: "Nine short stories featuring Hercule Poirot"
—Provided by publisher.
ISBN 978-1-62899-129-1 (library binding : alk. paper)
1. Poirot, Hercule (Fictitious character)—Fiction.
  2. Private investigators—England—Fiction. 3. Large type books.
  I. Title.
PR6005.H66U47 2014
823′.912—dc23

2014012968

Contents

1 The Under Dog   9

2 The Plymouth Express   103

3 The Affair at the Victory Ball   127

4 The Market Basing Mystery   151

5 The Lemesurier Inheritance   167

6 The Cornish Mystery   187

7 The King of Clubs   211

8 The Submarine Plans   237

9 The Adventure of the Clapham Cook   261

THE UNDER DOG
AND OTHER STORIES

One

The Under Dog

"The Under Dog" was first published in
the USA in *Mystery Magazine*, 1 April 1926,
then in *London Magazine*, October 1926.

Lily Margrave smoothed her gloves out on
her knee with a nervous gesture, and darted a
glance at the occupant of the big chair opposite
her.

She had heard of M. Hercule Poirot, the well-
known investigator, but this was the first time she
had seen him in the flesh.

The comic, almost ridiculous, aspect that he
presented disturbed her conception of him. Could
this funny little man, with the egg-shaped head
and the enormous moustaches, really do the
wonderful things that were claimed for him? His
occupation at the moment struck her as particularly childish. He was piling small blocks of
coloured wood one upon the other, and seemed
far more interested in the result than in the story
she was telling.

At her sudden silence, however, he looked
sharply across at her.

"Mademoiselle, continue, I pray of you. It is not

that I do not attend; I attend very carefully, I assure you."

He began once more to pile the little blocks of wood one upon the other, while the girl's voice took up the tale again. It was a gruesome tale, a tale of violence and tragedy, but the voice was so calm and unemotional, the recital was so concise that something of the savour of humanity seemed to have been left out of it.

She stopped at last.

"I hope," she said anxiously, "that I have made everything clear."

Poirot nodded his head several times in emphatic assent. Then he swept his hand across the wooden blocks, scattering them over the table, and, leaning back in his chair, his fingertips pressed together and his eyes on the ceiling, he began to recapitulate.

"Sir Reuben Astwell was murdered ten days ago. On Wednesday, the day before yesterday, his nephew, Charles Leverson, was arrested by the police. The facts against him as far as you know are:—you will correct me if I am wrong, Mademoiselle—Sir Reuben was sitting up late writing in his own special sanctum, the Tower room. Mr. Leverson came in late, letting himself in with a latch-key. He was overheard quarrelling with his uncle by the butler, whose room is directly below the Tower room. The quarrel ended with a sudden thud as of a chair being thrown over and a half-smothered cry.

"The butler was alarmed, and thought of getting up to see what was the matter, but as a few seconds later he heard Mr. Leverson leave the room gaily whistling a tune, he thought nothing more of it. On the following morning, however, a housemaid discovered Sir Reuben dead by his desk. He had been struck down by some heavy instrument. The butler, I gather, did not at once tell his story to the police. That was natural, I think, eh, Mademoiselle?"

The sudden question made Lily Margrave start.

"I beg your pardon?" she said.

"One looks for humanity in these matters, does one not?" said the little man. "As you recited the story to me—so admirably, so concisely—you made of the actors in the drama machines—puppets. But me, I look always for human nature. I say to myself, this butler, this—what did you say his name was?"

"His name is Parsons."

"This Parsons, then, he will have the characteristics of his class, he will object very strongly to the police, he will tell them as little as possible. Above all, he will say nothing that might seem to incriminate a member of the household. A house-breaker, a burglar, he will cling to that idea with all the strength of extreme obstinacy. Yes, the loyalties of the servant class are an interesting study."

He leaned back beaming.

"In the meantime," he went on, "everyone in the household has told his or her tale, Mr. Leverson among the rest, and his tale was that he had come in late and gone up to bed without seeing his uncle."

"That is what he said."

"And no one saw reason to doubt that tale," mused Poirot, "except, of course, Parsons. Then there comes down an inspector from Scotland Yard, Inspector Miller you said, did you not? I know him, I have come across him once or twice in the past. He is what they call the sharp man, the ferret, the weasel.

"Yes, I know him! And the sharp Inspector Miller, he sees what the local inspector has not seen, that Parsons is ill at ease and uncomfortable, and knows something that he has not told. *Eh bien*, he makes short work of Parsons. By now it has been clearly proved that no one broke into the house that night, that the murderer must be looked for inside the house and not outside. And Parsons is unhappy and frightened, and feels very relieved to have his secret knowledge drawn out of him.

"He has done his best to avoid scandal, but there are limits; and so Inspector Miller listens to Parsons' story, and asks a question or two, and then makes some private investigations of his own. The case he builds up is very strong—very strong.

"Blood-stained fingers rested on the corner of the chest in the Tower room, and the fingerprints were those of Charles Leverson. The housemaid told him she emptied a basin of bloodstained water in Mr. Leverson's room the morning after the crime. He explained to her that he had cut his finger, and he *had* a little cut there, oh yes, but such a very little cut! The cuff of his evening shirt had been washed, but they found bloodstains in the sleeve of his coat. He was hard pressed for money, and he inherited money at Sir Reuben's death. Oh, yes, a very strong case, Mademoiselle." He paused.

"And yet you come to me today."

Lily Margrave shrugged her slender shoulders.

"As I told you, M. Poirot, Lady Astwell sent me."

"You would not have come of your own accord, eh?"

The little man glanced at her shrewdly. The girl did not answer.

"You do not reply to my question."

Lily Margrave began smoothing her gloves again.

"It is rather difficult for me, M. Poirot. I have my loyalty to Lady Astwell to consider. Strictly speaking, I am only her paid companion, but she has treated me more as though I were a daughter or a niece. She has been extraordinarily kind and, whatever her faults, I should not like to appear to criticize her actions, or—well, to prejudice you against taking up the case."

"Impossible to prejudice Hercule Poirot, *cela ne ce fait pas*," declared the little man cheerily. "I perceive that you think Lady Astwell has in her bonnet the buzzing bee. Come now, is it not so?"

"If I must say—"

"Speak, Mademoiselle."

"I think the whole thing is simply silly."

"It strikes you like that, eh?"

"I don't want to say anything against Lady Astwell—"

"I comprehend," murmured Poirot gently. "I comprehend perfectly." His eyes invited her to go on.

"She really is a very good sort, and frightfully kind, but she isn't—how can I put it? She isn't an educated woman. You know she was an actress when Sir Reuben married her, and she has all sorts of prejudices and superstitions. If she says a thing, it must be so, and she simply won't listen to reason. The inspector was not very tactful with her, and it put her back up. She says it is nonsense to suspect Mr. Leverson and just the sort of stupid, pigheaded mistake the police would make, and that, of course, dear Charles did not do it."

"But she has no reasons, eh?"

"None whatever."

"Ha! Is that so? Really, now."

"I told her," said Lily, "that it would be no good

coming to you with a mere statement like that and nothing to go on."

"You told her that," said Poirot, "did you really? That is interesting."

His eyes swept over Lily Margrave in a quick comprehensive survey, taking in the details of her neat black suit, the touch of white at her throat and the smart little black hat. He saw the elegance of her, the pretty face with its slightly pointed chin, and the dark-blue, long-lashed eyes. Insensibly his attitude changed; he was interested now, not so much in the case as in the girl sitting opposite him.

"Lady Astwell is, I should imagine, Mademoiselle, just a trifle inclined to be unbalanced and hysterical?"

Lily Margrave nodded eagerly.

"That describes her exactly. She is, as I told you, very kind, but it is impossible to argue with her or to make her see things logically."

"Possibly she suspects someone on her own account," suggested Poirot, "someone quite absurd."

"That is exactly what she does do," cried Lily. "She has taken a great dislike to Sir Reuben's secretary, poor man. She says she *knows* he did it, and yet it has been proved quite conclusively that poor Owen Trefusis cannot possibly have done it."

"And she has no reasons?"

"Of course not; it is all intuition with her."

Lily Margrave's voice was very scornful.

"I perceive, Mademoiselle," said Poirot, smiling, "that you do not believe in intuition?"

"I think it is nonsense," replied Lily.

Poirot leaned back in his chair.

"*Les femmes*," he murmured, "they like to think that it is a special weapon that the good God has given them, and for every once that it shows them the truth, at least nine times it leads them astray."

"I know," said Lily, "but I have told you what Lady Astwell is like. You simply cannot argue with her."

"So you, Mademoiselle, being wise and discreet, came along to me as you were bidden, and have managed to put me *au courant* of the situation."

Something in the tone of his voice made the girl look up sharply.

"Of course, I know," said Lily apologetically, "how very valuable your time is."

"You are too flattering, Mademoiselle," said Poirot, "but indeed—yes, it is true, at this present time I have many cases of moment on hand."

"I was afraid that might be so," said Lily, rising. "I will tell Lady Astwell—"

But Poirot did not rise also. Instead he lay back in his chair and looked steadily up at the girl.

"You are in haste to be gone, Mademoiselle? Sit down one more little moment, I pray of you."

He saw the colour flood into her face and ebb out again. She sat down once more slowly and unwillingly.

"Mademoiselle is quick and decisive," said Poirot. "She must make allowances for an old man like myself, who comes to his decisions slowly. You mistook me, Mademoiselle. I did not say that I would not go down to Lady Astwell."

"You will come, then?"

The girl's tone was flat. She did not look at Poirot, but down at the ground, and so was unaware of the keen scrutiny with which he regarded her.

"Tell Lady Astwell, Mademoiselle, that I am entirely at her service. I will be at—Mon Repos, is it not?—this afternoon."

He rose. The girl followed suit.

"I—I will tell her. It is very good of you to come, M. Poirot. I am afraid, though, you will find you have been brought on a wild goose chase."

"Very likely, but—who knows?"

He saw her out with punctilious courtesy to the door. Then he returned to the sitting room, frowning, deep in thought. Once or twice he nodded his head, then he opened the door and called to his valet.

"My good George, prepare me, I pray of you, a little valise. I go down to the country this afternoon."

"Very good, sir," said George.

He was an extremely English-looking person. Tall, cadaverous and unemotional.

"A young girl is a very interesting phenomenon, George," said Poirot, as he dropped once more into his armchair and lighted a tiny cigarette. "Especially, you understand, when she has brains. To ask someone to do a thing and at the same time to put them against doing it, that is a delicate operation. It requires finesse. She was very adroit—oh, very adroit—but Hercule Poirot, my good George, is of a cleverness quite exceptional."

"I have heard you say so, sir."

"It is not the secretary she has in mind," mused Poirot. "Lady Astwell's accusation of him she treats with contempt. Just the same she is anxious that no one should disturb the sleeping dogs. I, my good George, I go to disturb them, I go to make the dog fight! There is a drama there, at Mon Repos. A human drama, and it excites me. She was adroit, the little one, but not adroit enough. I wonder—I wonder what I shall find there?"

Into the dramatic pause which succeeded these words George's voice broke apologetically:

"Shall I pack dress clothes, sir?"

Poirot looked at him sadly.

"Always the concentration, the attention to your own job. You are very good for me, George."

●　●　●

When the 4:55 drew up at Abbots Cross station, there descended from it M. Hercule Poirot, very neatly and foppishly attired, his moustaches waxed to a stiff point. He gave up his ticket, passed through the barrier, and was accosted by a tall chauffeur.

"M. Poirot?"

The little man beamed upon him.

"That is my name."

"This way, sir, if you please."

He held open the door of the big Rolls-Royce.

The house was a bare three minutes from the station. The chauffeur descended once more and opened the door of the car, and Poirot stepped out. The butler was already holding the front door open.

Poirot gave the outside of the house a swift appraising glance before passing through the open door. It was a big, solidly built red-brick mansion, with no pretensions to beauty, but with an air of solid comfort.

Poirot stepped into the hall. The butler relieved him deftly of his hat and overcoat, then murmured with that deferential undertone only to be achieved by the best servants:

"Her ladyship is expecting you, sir."

Poirot followed the butler up the soft-carpeted stairs. This, without doubt, was Parsons, a very well-trained servant, with a manner suitably devoid of emotion. At the top of the staircase he turned to the right along a corridor. He passed through a door into a little anteroom, from which two more doors led. He threw open the left-hand one of these, and announced:

"M. Poirot, m'lady."

The room was not a very large one, and it was crowded with furniture and knickknacks. A woman, dressed in black, got up from a sofa and came quickly towards Poirot.

"M. Poirot," she said with outstretched hand. Her eye ran rapidly over the dandified figure. She paused a minute, ignoring the little man's bow over her hand, and his murmured "Madame," and then, releasing his hand after a sudden vigorous pressure, she exclaimed:

"I believe in small men! They are the clever ones."

"Inspector Miller," murmured Poirot, "is, I think, a tall man?"

"He is a bumptious idiot," said Lady Astwell. "Sit down here by me, will you, M. Poirot?"

She indicated the sofa and went on:

"Lily did her best to put me off sending for you, but I have not come to my time of life without knowing my own mind."

"A rare accomplishment," said Poirot, as he followed her to the settee.

Lady Astwell settled herself comfortably among the cushions and turned so as to face him.

"Lily is a dear girl," said Lady Astwell, "but she thinks she knows everything, and as often as not in my experience those sort of people are wrong. I am not clever, M. Poirot, I never have been, but I am right where many a more stupid person is wrong. I believe in *guidance*. Now do you want me to tell you who is the murderer, or do you not? A woman knows, M. Poirot."

"Does Miss Margrave know?"

"What did she tell you?" asked Lady Astwell sharply.

"She gave me the facts of the case."

"The facts? Oh, of course they are dead against Charles, but I tell you, M. Poirot, he didn't do it. I *know* he didn't!" She bent upon him an earnestness that was almost disconcerting.

"You are very positive, Lady Astwell?"

"Trefusis killed my husband, M. Poirot. I am sure of it."

"Why?"

"Why should he kill him, do you mean, or why am I sure? I tell you I *know* it! I am funny about those things. I make up my mind at once, and I stick to it."

"Did Mr. Trefusis benefit in any way by Sir Reuben's death?"

"Never left him a penny," returned Lady Astwell promptly. "Now that shows you dear Reuben couldn't have liked or trusted him."

"Had he been with Sir Reuben long, then?"

"Close on nine years."

"That is a long time," said Poirot softly, "a very long time to remain in the employment of one man. Yes, Mr. Trefusis, he must have known his employer well."

Lady Astwell stared at him.

"What are you driving at? I don't see what that has to do with it."

"I was following out a little idea of my own," said Poirot. "A little idea, not interesting, perhaps, but original, on the effects of service."

Lady Astwell still stared.

"You *are* very clever, aren't you?" she said in rather a doubtful tone. "Everybody says so."

Hercule Poirot laughed.

"Perhaps you shall pay me that compliment, too, Madame, one of these days. But let us return to the motive. Tell me now of your household, of the people who were here in the house on the day of the tragedy."

"There was Charles, of course."

"He was your husband's nephew, I understand, not yours."

"Yes, Charles was the only son of Reuben's sister. She married a comparatively rich man, but one of those crashes came—they do, in the city—and he died, and his wife, too, and Charles came to live with us. He was twenty-three at the time, and going to be a barrister. But when the trouble came, Reuben took him into his office."

"He was industrious, M. Charles?"

"I like a man who is quick on the uptake," said Lady Astwell with a nod of approval. "No, that's just the trouble, Charles was *not* industrious. He was always having rows with his uncle over some muddle or other that he had made. Not that poor Reuben was an easy man to get on with. Many's the time I've told him he had forgotten what it was to be young himself. He was very different in those days, M. Poirot."

Lady Astwell heaved a sigh of reminiscence.

"Changes must come, Madame," said Poirot. "It is the law."

"Still," said Lady Astwell, "he was never really rude to *me*. At least if he was, he was always sorry afterwards—poor dear Reuben."

"He was difficult, eh?" said Poirot.

"I could always manage him," said Lady Astwell with the air of a successful lion tamer. "But it was rather awkward sometimes when he would lose his temper with the servants. There are ways of doing that, and Reuben's was not the right way."

"How exactly did Sir Reuben leave his money, Lady Astwell?"

"Half to me and half to Charles," replied Lady Astwell promptly. "The lawyers don't put it simply like that, but that's what it amounts to."

Poirot nodded his head.

"I see—I see," he murmured. "Now, Lady

Astwell, I will demand of you that you will describe to me the household. There was yourself, and Sir Reuben's nephew, Mr. Charles Leverson, and the secretary, Mr. Owen Trefusis, and there was Miss Lily Margrave. Perhaps you will tell me something of that young lady."

"You want to know about Lily?"

"Yes, she had been with you long?"

"About a year. I have had a lot of secretary-companions you know, but somehow or other they all got on my nerves. Lily was different. She was tactful and full of common sense and besides she looks so nice. I do like to have a pretty face about me, M. Poirot. I am a funny kind of person; I take likes and dislikes straight away. As soon as I saw that girl, I said to myself: 'She'll do.'"

"Did she come to you through friends, Lady Astwell?"

"I think she answered an advertisement. Yes—that was it."

"You know something of her people, of where she comes from?"

"Her father and mother are out in India, I believe. I don't really know much about them, but you can see at a glance that Lily is a lady, can't you, M. Poirot?"

"Oh, perfectly, perfectly."

"Of course," went on Lady Astwell, "I am not a lady myself. I know it, and the servants know it, but there is nothing mean-spirited about me. I can appreciate the real thing when I see it, and no one could be nicer than Lily has been to me. I look upon that girl almost as a daughter, M. Poirot, indeed I do."

Poirot's right hand strayed out and straightened one or two of the objects lying on a table near him.

"Did Sir Reuben share this feeling?" he asked.

His eyes were on the knickknacks, but doubtless he noted the pause before Lady Astwell's answer came.

"With a man it's different. Of course they—they got on very well."

"Thank you, Madame," said Poirot. He was smiling to himself.

"And these were the only people in the house that night?" he asked. "Excepting, of course, the servants."

"Oh, there was Victor."

"Victor?"

"Yes, my husband's brother, you know, and his partner."

"He lived with you?"

"No, he had just arrived on a visit. He has been out in West Africa for the past few years."

"West Africa," murmured Poirot.

He had learned that Lady Astwell could be trusted to develop a subject herself if sufficient time was given her.

"They say it's a wonderful country, but I think it's the kind of place that has a very bad effect upon a man. They drink too much, and they get uncontrolled. None of the Astwells has a good temper, and Victor's, since he came back from Africa, has been simply too shocking. He has frightened *me* once or twice."

"Did he frighten Miss Margrave, I wonder?" murmured Poirot gently.

"Lily? Oh, I don't think he has seen much of Lily."

Poirot made a note or two in a diminutive notebook; then he put the pencil back in its loop and returned the notebook to his pocket.

"I thank you, Lady Astwell. I will now, if I may, interview Parsons."

"Will you have him up here?"

Lady Astwell's hand moved towards the bell. Poirot arrested the gesture quickly.

"No, no, a thousand times no. I will descend to him."

"If you think it is better—"

Lady Astwell was clearly disappointed at not being able to participate in the forthcoming scene. Poirot adopted an air of secrecy.

"It is essential," he said mysteriously, and left Lady Astwell duly impressed.

He found Parsons in the butler's pantry, polishing silver. Poirot opened the proceedings with one of his funny little bows.

"I must explain myself," he said. "I am a detective agent."

"Yes, sir," said Parsons, "we gathered as much." His tone was respectful but aloof.

"Lady Astwell sent for me," continued Poirot. "She is not satisfied; no, she is not satisfied at all."

"I have heard her ladyship say so on several occasions," said Parsons.

"In fact," said Poirot, "I recount to you the things you already know? Eh? Let us then not waste time on these bagatelles. Take me, if you will be so good, to your bedroom and tell me exactly what it was you heard there on the night of the murder."

The butler's room was on the ground floor, adjoining the servants' hall. It had barred windows, and the strong-room was in one corner of it. Parsons indicated the narrow bed.

"I had retired, sir, at eleven o'clock. Miss Margrave had gone to bed, and Lady Astwell was with Sir Reuben in the Tower room."

"Lady Astwell was with Sir Reuben? Ah, proceed."

"The Tower room, sir, is directly over this. If people are talking in it one can hear the murmur of voices, but naturally not anything that is said. I must have fallen asleep about half past eleven. It was just twelve o'clock when I was awakened by the sound of the front door being slammed to and knew Mr. Leverson had returned. Presently I heard footsteps overhead, and a minute or two

27

later Mr. Leverson's voice talking to Sir Reuben.

"It was my fancy at the time, sir, that Mr. Leverson was—I should not exactly like to say drunk, but inclined to be a little indiscreet and noisy. He was shouting at his uncle at the top of his voice. I caught a word or two here or there, but not enough to understand what it was all about, and then there was a sharp cry and a heavy thud."

There was a pause, and Parsons repeated the last words.

"A heavy thud," he said impressively.

"If I mistake not, it is a *dull* thud in most works of romance," murmured Poirot.

"Maybe, sir," said Parsons severely. "It was a *heavy* thud I heard."

"A thousand pardons," said Poirot.

"Do not mention it, sir. After the thud, in the silence, I heard Mr. Leverson's voice as plain as plain can be, raised high. 'My God,' he said, 'my God,' just like that, sir."

Parsons, from his first reluctance to tell the tale, had now progressed to a thorough enjoyment of it. He fancied himself mightily as a narrator. Poirot played up to him.

"*Mon Dieu*," he murmured. "What emotion you must have experienced!"

"Yes, indeed, sir," said Parsons, "as you say, sir. Not that I thought very much of it at the time. But it *did* occur to me to wonder if anything was amiss, and whether I had better go up and see. I went to turn the electric light on, and was unfortunate enough to knock over a chair.

"I opened the door, and went through the servants' hall, and opened the other door which gives on a passage. The back stairs lead up from there, and as I stood at the bottom of them, hesitating, I heard Mr. Leverson's voice from up above, speaking hearty and cheery-like. 'No harm done, luckily,' he says. 'Good night,' and I heard him move off along the passage to his own room, whistling.

"Of course I went back to bed at once. Just something knocked over, that's all I thought it was. I ask you, sir, was I to think Sir Reuben was murdered, with Mr. Leverson saying good night and all?"

"You are sure it was Mr. Leverson's voice you heard?"

Parsons looked at the little Belgian pityingly, and Poirot saw clearly enough that, right or wrong, Parsons' mind was made up on this point.

"Is there anything further you would like to ask me, sir?"

"There is one thing," said Poirot, "do you like Mr. Leverson?"

"I—I beg your pardon, sir?"

"It is a simple question. Do you like Mr. Leverson?"

Parsons, from being startled at first, now seemed embarrassed.

"The general opinion in the servants' hall, sir," he said, and paused.

"By all means," said Poirot, "put it that way if it pleases you."

"The opinion is, sir, that Mr. Leverson is an open-handed young gentleman, but not, if I may say so, particularly intelligent, sir."

"Ah!" said Poirot. "Do you know, Parsons, that without having seen him, that is also precisely my opinion of Mr. Leverson."

"Indeed, sir."

"What is your opinion—I beg your pardon—the opinion of the servants' hall of the secretary?"

"He is a very quiet, patient gentleman, sir. Anxious to give no trouble."

"*Vraiment*," said Poirot.

The butler coughed.

"Her ladyship, sir," he murmured, "is apt to be a little hasty in her judgments."

"Then, in the opinion of the servants' hall, Mr. Leverson committed the crime?"

"We none of us wish to think it was Mr. Leverson," said Parsons. "We—well, plainly, we didn't think he had it in him, sir."

"But he has a somewhat violent temper, has he not?" asked Poirot.

Parsons came nearer to him.

"If you are asking me who had the most violent temper in the house—"

Poirot held up a hand.

"Ah! But that is not the question I should ask," he said softly. "My question would be, who has the best temper?" Parsons stared at him open-mouthed.

Poirot wasted no further time on him. With an amiable little bow—he was always amiable—he left the room and wandered out into the big square hall of Mon Repos. There he stood a minute or two in thought, then, at a slight sound that came to him, cocked his head on one side in the manner of a perky robin, and finally, with noiseless steps, crossed to one of the doors that led out of the hall.

He stood in the doorway, looking into the room; a small room furnished as a library. At a big desk at the farther end of it sat a thin, pale young man busily writing. He had a receding chin, and wore pince-nez.

Poirot watched him for some minutes, and then he broke the silence by giving a completely artificial and theatrical cough.

"Ahem!" coughed M. Hercule Poirot.

The young man at the desk stopped writing and turned his head. He did not appear unduly startled, but an expression of perplexity gathered on his face as he eyed Poirot.

The latter came forward with a little bow.

"I have the honour of speaking to M. Trefusis, yes? Ah! My name is Poirot, Hercule Poirot. You may perhaps have heard of me."

31

"Oh—er—yes, certainly," said the young man.

Poirot eyed him attentively.

Owen Trefusis was about thirty-three years of age, and the detective saw at once why nobody was inclined to treat Lady Astwell's accusation seriously. Mr. Owen Trefusis was a prim, proper young man, disarmingly meek, the type of man who can be, and is, systematically bullied. One could feel quite sure that he would never display resentment.

"Lady Astwell sent for you, of course," said the secretary. "She mentioned that she was going to do so. Is there any way in which I can help you?"

His manner was polite without being effusive. Poirot accepted a chair, and murmured gently:

"Has Lady Astwell said anything to you of her beliefs and suspicions?"

Owen Trefusis smiled a little.

"As far as that goes," he said, "I believe she suspects me. It is absurd, but there it is. She has hardly spoken a civil word to me since Sir Reuben's death, and she shrinks against the wall as I pass by."

His manner was perfectly natural, and there was more amusement than resentment in his voice. Poirot nodded with an air of engaging frankness.

"Between ourselves," he explained, "she said the same thing to me. I did not argue with her—me, I have made it a rule never to argue with very positive ladies. You comprehend, it is a waste of time."

"Oh, quite."

"I say, yes, Madame—oh, perfectly, Madame— *précisément*, Madame. They mean nothing, those words, but they soothe all the same. I make my investigations, for though it seems almost impossible that anyone except M. Leverson could have committed the crime, yet—well, the impossible has happened before now."

"I understand your position perfectly," said the secretary. "Please regard me as entirely at your service."

"*Bon*," said Poirot. "We understand one another. Now recount to me the events of that evening. Better start with dinner."

"Leverson was not at dinner, as you doubtless know," said the secretary. "He had a serious disagreement with his uncle, and went off to dine at the golf club. Sir Reuben was in a very bad temper in consequence."

"Not too amiable, *ce Monsieur*, eh?" hinted Poirot delicately.

Trefusis laughed.

"Oh! He was a Tartar! I haven't worked with him for nine years without knowing most of his little ways. He was an extraordinarily difficult man, M. Poirot. He would get into childish fits of rage and abuse anybody who came near him.

"I was used to it by that time. I got into the habit

of paying absolutely no attention to anything he said. He was not bad-hearted really, but he could be most foolish and exasperating in his manner. The great thing was never to answer him back."

"Were other people as wise as you were in that respect?"

Trefusis shrugged his shoulders.

"Lady Astwell enjoyed a good row," he said. "She was not in the least afraid of Sir Reuben, and she always stood up to him and gave him as good as she got. They always made it up afterwards, and Sir Reuben was really devoted to her."

"Did they quarrel that night?"

The secretary looked at him sideways, hesitated a minute, then he said:

"I believe so; what made you ask?"

"An idea, that is all."

"I don't know, of course," explained the secretary, "but things looked as though they were working up that way."

Poirot did not pursue the topic.

"Who else was at dinner?"

"Miss Margrave, Mr. Victor Astwell, and myself."

"And afterwards?"

"We went into the drawing room. Sir Reuben did not accompany us. About ten minutes later he came in and hauled me over the coals for some trifling matter about a letter. I went up with him to the Tower room and set the thing straight; then

Mr. Victor Astwell came in and said he had something he wished to talk to his brother about, so I went downstairs and joined the two ladies.

"About a quarter of an hour later I heard Sir Reuben's bell ringing violently, and Parsons came to say I was to go up to Sir Reuben at once. As I entered the room, Mr. Victor Astwell was coming out. He nearly knocked me over. Something had evidently happened to upset him. He has a very violent temper. I really believe he didn't see me."

"Did Sir Reuben make any comment on the matter?"

"He said: 'Victor is a lunatic; he will do for somebody some day when he is in one of these rages.'"

"Ah!" said Poirot. "Have you any idea what the trouble was about?"

"I couldn't say at all."

Poirot turned his head very slowly and looked at the secretary. Those last words had been uttered too hastily. He formed the conviction that Trefusis could have said more had he wished to do so. But once again Poirot did not press the question.

"And then? Proceed, I pray of you."

"I worked with Sir Reuben for about an hour and a half. At eleven o'clock Lady Astwell came in, and Sir Reuben told me I could go to bed."

"And you went?"

"Yes."

"Have you any idea how long she stayed with him?"

"None at all. Her room is on the first floor, and mine is on the second, so I would not hear her go to bed."

"I see."

Poirot nodded his head once or twice and sprang to his feet.

"And now, Monsieur, take me to the Tower room."

He followed the secretary up the broad stairs to the first landing. Here Trefusis led him along the corridor, and through a baize door at the end of it, which gave on the servants' staircase and on a short passage that ended in a door. They passed through this door and found themselves on the scene of the crime.

It was a lofty room twice as high as any of the others, and was roughly about thirty feet square. Swords and assagais adorned the walls, and many native curious were arranged about on tables. At the far end, in the embrasure of the window, was a large writing table. Poirot crossed straight to it.

"It was here Sir Reuben was found?"

Trefusis nodded.

"He was struck from behind, I understand?"

Again the secretary nodded.

"The crime was committed with one of these native clubs," he explained. "A tremendously heavy thing. Death must have been practically instantaneous."

"That strengthens the conviction that the crime was not premeditated. A sharp quarrel, and a weapon snatched up almost unconsciously."

"Yes, it does not look well for poor Leverson."

"And the body was found fallen forward on the desk?"

"No, it had slipped sideways to the ground."

"Ah," said Poirot, "that is curious."

"Why curious?" asked the secretary.

"Because of this."

Poirot pointed to a round irregular stain on the polished surface of the writing table.

"That is a bloodstain, *mon ami*."

"It may have spattered there," suggested Trefusis, "or it may have been made later, when they moved the body."

"Very possibly, very possibly," said the little man. "There is only the one door to this room?"

"There is a staircase here."

Trefusis pulled aside a velvet curtain in the corner of the room nearest the door, where a small spiral staircase led upwards.

"This place was originally built by an astronomer. The stairs led up to the tower where the telescope was fixed. Sir Reuben had the place fitted up as a bedroom, and sometimes slept there if he was working very late."

Poirot went nimbly up the stairs. The circular

room upstairs was plainly furnished, with a camp-bed, a chair and dressing table. Poirot satisfied himself that there was no other exit, and then came down again to where Trefusis stood waiting for him.

"Did you hear Mr. Leverson come in?" he asked.

Trefusis shook his head.

"I was fast asleep by that time."

Poirot nodded. He looked slowly round the room.

"*Eh bien!*" he said at last. "I do not think there is anything further here, unless—perhaps you would be so kind as to draw the curtains."

Obediently Trefusis pulled the heavy black curtains across the window at the far end of the room. Poirot switched on the light—which was masked by a big alabaster bowl hanging from the ceiling.

"There was a desk light?" he asked.

For reply the secretary clicked on a powerful green-shaded hand lamp, which stood on the writing table. Poirot switched the other light off, then on, then off again.

"*C'est bien!* I have finished here."

"Dinner is at half past seven," murmured the secretary.

"I thank you, M. Trefusis, for your many amiabilities."

"Not at all."

Poirot went thoughtfully along the corridor to the room appointed for him. The inscrutable George was there laying out his master's things.

"My good George," he said presently, "I shall, I hope, meet at dinner a certain gentleman who begins to intrigue me greatly. A man who has come home from the tropics, George. With a tropical temper—so it is said. A man whom Parsons tries to tell me about, and whom Lily Margrave does not mention. The late Sir Reuben had a temper of his own, George. Supposing such a man to come into contact with a man whose temper was worse than his own—how do you say it? The fur would jump about, eh?"

" 'Would fly' is the correct expression, sir, and it is not always the case, sir, not by a long way."

"No?"

"No, sir. There was my Aunt Jemima, sir, a most shrewish tongue she had, bullied a poor sister of hers who lived with her, something shocking she did. Nearly worried the life out of her. But if anyone came along who stood up to her, well, it was a very different thing. It was meekness she couldn't bear."

"Ha!" said Poirot, "it is suggestive—that."

George coughed apologetically.

"Is there anything I can do in any way," he inquired delicately, "to—er—assist you, sir?"

"Certainly," said Poirot promptly. "You can find out for me what colour evening dress Miss

Lily Margrave wore that night, and which housemaid attends her."

George received these commands with his usual stolidity.

"Very good, sir, I will have the information for you in the morning."

Poirot rose from his seat and stood gazing into the fire.

"You are very useful to me, George," he murmured. "Do you know, I shall not forget your Aunt Jemima?"

Poirot did not, after all, see Victor Astwell that night. A telephone message came from him that he was detained in London.

"He attends to the affairs of your late husband's business, eh?" asked Poirot of Lady Astwell.

"Victor is a partner," she explained. "He went out to Africa to look into some mining concessions for the firm. It *was* mining, wasn't it, Lily?"

"Yes, Lady Astwell."

"Gold mines, I think, or was it copper or tin? You ought to know, Lily, you were always asking Reuben questions about it all. Oh, do be careful, dear, you will have that vase over!"

"It is dreadfully hot in here with the fire," said the girl. "Shall I—shall I open the window a little?"

"If you like, dear," said Lady Astwell placidly.

Poirot watched while the girl went across to the

40

window and opened it. She stood there a minute or two breathing in the cool night air. When she returned and sat down in her seat, Poirot said to her politely:

"So Mademoiselle is interested in mines?"

"Oh, not really," said the girl indifferently. "I listened to Sir Reuben, but I don't know anything about the subject."

"You pretended very well, then," said Lady Astwell. "Poor Reuben actually thought you had some ulterior motive in asking all those questions."

The little detective's eyes had not moved from the fire, into which he was steadily staring, but nevertheless, he did not miss the quick flush of vexation on Lily Margrave's face. Tactfully he changed the conversation. When the hour for good nights came, Poirot said to his hostess:

"May I have just two little words with you, Madame?"

Lily Margrave vanished discreetly. Lady Astwell looked inquiringly at the detective.

"You were the last person to see Sir Reuben alive that night?"

She nodded. Tears sprang into her eyes, and she hastily held a black-edged handkerchief to them.

"Ah, do not distress yourself, I beg of you do not distress yourself."

"It's all very well, M. Poirot, but I can't help it."

41

"I am a triple imbecile thus to vex you."

"No, no, go on. What were you going to say?"

"It was about eleven o'clock, I fancy, when you went into the Tower room, and Sir Reuben dismissed Mr. Trefusis. Is that right?"

"It must have been about then."

"How long were you with him?"

"It was just a quarter to twelve when I got up to my room; I remember glancing at the clock."

"Lady Astwell, will you tell me what your conversation with your husband was about?"

Lady Astwell sank down on the sofa and broke down completely. Her sobs were vigorous.

"We—qua—qua—quarrelled," she moaned.

"What about?" Poirot's voice was coaxing, almost tender.

"L-l-lots of things. It b-b-began with L-Lily. Reuben took a dislike to her—for no reason, and said he had caught her interfering with his papers. He wanted to send her away, and I said she was a dear girl, and I would not have it. And then he s-s-started shouting me down, and I wouldn't have that, so I just told him what I thought of him.

"Not that I really meant it, M. Poirot. He said he had taken me out of the gutter to marry me, and I said—ah, but what does it all matter now? I shall never forgive myself. You know how it is, M. Poirot, I always did say a good row clears the air, and how was I to know someone was going to murder him that very night? Poor old Reuben."

Poirot had listened sympathetically to all this outburst.

"I have caused you suffering," he said. "I apologize. Let us now be very businesslike—very practical, very exact. You still cling to your idea that Mr. Trefusis murdered your husband?"

Lady Astwell drew herself up.

"A woman's instinct, M. Poirot," she said solemnly, "never lies."

"Exactly, exactly," said Poirot. "But when did he do it?"

"When? After I left him, of course."

"You left Sir Reuben at a quarter to twelve. At five minutes to twelve Mr. Leverson came in. In that ten minutes you say the secretary came along from his bedroom and murdered him?"

"It is perfectly possible."

"So many things are possible," said Poirot. "It could be done in ten minutes. Oh, yes! But was it?"

"Of course he *says* he was in bed and fast asleep," said Lady Astwell, "but who is to know if he was or not?"

"Nobody saw him about," Poirot reminded her.

"Everybody was in bed and fast asleep," said Lady Astwell triumphantly. "Of course nobody saw him."

"I wonder," said Poirot to himself.

A short pause.

"*Eh bien*, Lady Astwell, I wish you good night."

George deposited a tray of early-morning coffee by his master's bedside.

"Miss Margrave, sir, wore a dress of light green chiffon on the night in question."

"Thank you, George, you are most reliable."

"The third housemaid looks after Miss Margrave, sir. Her name is Gladys."

"Thank you, George. You are invaluable."

"Not at all, sir."

"It is a fine morning," said Poirot, looking out of the window, "and no one is likely to be astir very early. I think, my good George, that we shall have the Tower room to ourselves if we proceed there to make a little experiment."

"You need me, sir?"

"The experiment," said Poirot, "will not be painful."

The curtains were still drawn in the Tower room when they arrived there. George was about to pull them, when Poirot restrained him.

"We will leave the room as it is. Just turn on the desk lamp."

The valet obeyed.

"Now, my good George, sit down in that chair. Dispose yourself as though you were writing. *Très bien.* Me, I seize a club, I steal up behind you, so, and I hit you on the back of the head."

"Yes, sir," said George.

"Ah!" said Poirot, "but when I hit you, do not

continue to write. You comprehend I cannot be exact. I cannot hit you with the same force with which the assassin hit Sir Reuben. When it comes to that point, we must do the make-believe. I hit you on the head, and you collapse, so. The arms well relaxed, the body limp. Permit me to arrange you. But no, do not flex your muscles."

He heaved a sigh of exasperation.

"You press admirably the trousers, George," he said, "but the imagination you possess it not. Get up and let me take your place."

Poirot in his turn sat down at the writing table.

"I write," he declared, "I write busily. You steal up behind me, you hit me on the head with the club. Crash! The pen slips from my fingers, I drop forward, but not very far forward, for the chair is low, and the desk is high, and, moreover, my arms support me. Have the goodness, George, to go back to the door, stand there, and tell me what you see."

"Ahem!"

"Yes, George?" encouragingly.

"I see you, sir, sitting at the desk."

"*Sitting* at the desk?"

"It is a little difficult to see plainly, sir," explained George, "being such a long way away, sir, and the lamp being so heavily shaded. If I might turn on this light, sir?"

His hand reached out to the switch.

"Not at all," said Poirot sharply. "We shall do

very well as we are. Here am I bending over the desk, there are you standing by the door. Advance now, George, advance, and put your hand on my shoulder."

George obeyed.

"Lean on me a little, George, to steady yourself on your feet, as it were. Ah! *Voilà.*"

Hercule Poirot's limp body slid artistically sideways.

"I collapse—so!" he observed. "Yes, it is very well imagined. There is now something most important that must be done."

"Indeed, sir?" said the valet.

"Yes, it is necessary that I should breakfast well."

The little man laughed heartily at his own joke.

"The stomach, George; it must not be ignored."

George maintained a disapproving silence. Poirot went downstairs chuckling happily to himself. He was pleased at the way things were shaping. After breakfast he made the acquaintance of Gladys, the third housemaid. He was very interested in what she could tell him of the crime. She was sympathetic towards Charles, although she had no doubt of his guilt.

"Poor young gentleman, sir, it seems hard, it does, him not being quite himself at the time."

"He and Miss Margrave should have got on well together," suggested Poirot, "as the only two young people in the house."

Gladys shook her head.

"Very stand-offish Miss Lily was with him. She wouldn't have no carryings-on, and she made it plain."

"He was fond of her, was he?"

"Oh, only in passing, so to speak; no harm in it, sir. Mr. Victor Astwell, now he *is* properly gone on Miss Lily."

She giggled.

"Ah *vraiment!*"

Gladys giggled again.

"Sweet on her straightaway he was. Miss Lily *is* just like a lily, isn't she, sir? So tall and such a lovely shade of gold hair."

"She should wear a green evening frock," mused Poirot. "There is a certain shade of green—"

"She has one, sir," said Gladys. "Of course, she can't wear it now, being in mourning, but she had it on the very night Sir Reuben died."

"It should be a light green, not a dark green," said Poirot.

"It is a light green, sir. If you wait a minute I'll show it to you. Miss Lily has just gone out with the dogs."

Poirot nodded. He knew that as well as Gladys did. In fact, it was only after seeing Lily safely off the premises that he had gone in search of the housemaid. Gladys hurried away, and returned a few minutes later with a green evening dress on a hanger.

"*Exquis*!" murmured Poirot, holding up hands of admiration. "Permit me to take it to the light a minute."

He took the dress from Gladys, turned his back on her and hurried to the window. He bent over it, then held it out at arm's length.

"It is perfect," he declared. "Perfectly ravishing. A thousand thanks for showing it to me."

"Not at all, sir," said Gladys. "We all know that Frenchmen are interested in ladies' dresses."

"You are too kind," murmured Poirot.

He watched her hurry away again with the dress. Then he looked down at his two hands and smiled. In the right hand was a tiny pair of nail scissors, in the left was a neatly clipped fragment of green chiffon.

"And now," he murmured, "to be heroic."

He returned to his own apartment and summoned George.

"On the dressing table, my good George, you will perceive a gold scarf pin."

"Yes, sir."

"On the washstand is a solution of carbolic. Immerse, I pray you, the point of the pin in the carbolic."

George did as he was bid. He had long ago ceased to wonder at the vagaries of his master.

"I have done that, sir."

"*Très bien*! Now approach. I tender to you my first finger; insert the point of the pin in it."

"Excuse me, sir, you want me to prick you, sir?"

"But yes, you have guessed correctly. You must draw blood, you understand, but not too much."

George took hold of his master's finger. Poirot shut his eyes and leaned back. The valet stabbed at the finger with the scarf pin, and Poirot uttered a shrill yell.

"*Je vous remercie*, George," he said. "What you have done is ample."

Taking a small piece of green chiffon from his pocket, he dabbed his finger with it gingerly.

"The operation has succeeded to a miracle," he remarked, gazing at the result. "You have no curiosity, George? Now, that is admirable!"

The valet had just taken a discreet look out of the window.

"Excuse me, sir," he murmured, "a gentleman has driven up in a large car."

"Ah! Ah!" said Poirot. He rose briskly to his feet. "The elusive Mr. Victor Astwell. I go down to make his acquaintance."

Poirot was destined to hear Mr. Victor Astwell some time before he saw him. A loud voice rang out from the hall.

"Mind what you are doing, you damned idiot! That case has got glass in it. Curse you, Parsons, get out of the way! Put it down, you fool!"

Poirot skipped nimbly down the stairs. Victor

Astwell was a big man. Poirot bowed to him politely.

"Who the devil are you?" roared the big man.

Poirot bowed again.

"My name is Hercule Poirot."

"Lord!" said Victor Astwell. "So Nancy sent for you, after all, did she?"

He put a hand on Poirot's shoulder and steered him into the library.

"So you are the fellow they make such a fuss about," he remarked, looking him up and down. "Sorry for my language just now. That chauffeur of mine is a damned ass, and Parsons always does get on my nerves, blithering old idiot.

"I don't suffer fools gladly, you know," he said, half-apologetically, "but by all accounts you are not a fool, eh, M. Poirot?"

He laughed breezily.

"Those who have thought so have been sadly mistaken," said Poirot placidly.

"Is that so? Well, so Nancy has carted you down here—got a bee in her bonnet about the secretary. There is nothing in that; Trefusis is as mild as milk—drinks milk, too, I believe. The fellow is a teetotaller. Rather a waste of your time isn't it?"

"If one has an opportunity to observe human nature, time is never wasted," said Poirot quietly.

"Human nature, eh?"

Victor Astwell stared at him, then he flung himself down in a chair.

"Anything I can do for you?"

"Yes, you can tell me what your quarrel with your brother was about that evening."

Victor Astwell shook his head.

"Nothing to do with the case," he said decisively.

"One can never be sure," said Poirot.

"It had nothing to do with Charles Leverson."

"Lady Astwell thinks that Charles had nothing to do with the murder."

"Oh, Nancy!"

"Parsons assumes that it was M. Charles Leverson who came in that night, but he didn't see him. Remember nobody saw him."

"It's very simple. Reuben had been pitching into young Charles—not without good reason, I must say. Later on he tried to bully me. I told him a few home truths and, just to annoy him, I made up my mind to back the boy. I meant to see him that night, so as to tell him how the land lay. When I went up to my room I didn't go to bed. Instead, I left the door ajar and sat on a chair smoking. My room is on the second floor, M. Poirot, and Charles's room is next to it."

"Pardon my interrupting you—Mr. Trefusis, he, too, sleeps on that floor?"

Astwell nodded.

"Yes, his room is just beyond mine."

"Nearer the stairs?"

"No, the other way."

A curious light came into Poirot's face, but the other didn't notice it and went on:

"As I say, I waited up for Charles. I heard the front door slam, as I thought, about five minutes to twelve, but there was no sign of Charles for about ten minutes. When he did come up the stairs I saw that it was no good tackling him that night."

He lifted his elbow significantly.

"I see," murmured Poirot.

"Poor devil couldn't walk straight," said Astwell. "He was looking pretty ghastly, too. I put it down to his condition at the time. Of course, now, I realize that he had come straight from committing the crime."

Poirot interposed a quick question.

"You heard nothing from the Tower room?"

"No, but you must remember that I was right at the other end of the building. The walls are thick, and I don't believe you would even hear a pistol shot fired from there."

Poirot nodded.

"I asked if he would like some help getting to bed," continued Astwell. "But he said he was all right and went into his room and banged the door. I undressed and went to bed."

Poirot was staring thoughtfully at the carpet.

"You realize, M. Astwell," he said at last, "that your evidence is very important?"

"I suppose so, at least—what do you mean?"

"Your evidence that ten minutes elapsed between the slamming of the front door and Leverson's appearance upstairs. He himself says, so I understand, that he came into the house and went straight up to bed. But there is more than that. Lady Astwell's accusation of the secretary is fantastic, I admit, yet up to now it has not been proved impossible. But your evidence creates an alibi."

"How is that?"

"Lady Astwell says that she left her husband at a quarter to twelve, while the secretary had gone to bed at eleven o'clock. The only time he could have committed the crime was between a quarter to twelve and Charles Leverson's return. Now, if, as you say, you sat with your door open, he could not have come out of his room without your seeing him."

"That is so," agreed the other.

"There is no other staircase?"

"No, to get down to the Tower room he would have had to pass my door, and he didn't, I am quite sure of that. And, anyway, M. Poirot, as I said just now, the man is as meek as a parson, I assure you."

"But yes, but yes," said Poirot soothingly, "I understand all that." He paused. "And you will not tell me the subject of your quarrel with Sir Reuben?"

The other's face turned a dark red.

"You'll get nothing out of me."

Poirot looked at the ceiling.

"I can always be discreet," he murmured, "where a lady is concerned."

Victor Astwell sprang to his feet.

"Damn you, how did you—what do you mean?"

"I was thinking," said Poirot, "of Miss Lily Margrave."

Victor Astwell stood undecided for a minute or two, then his colour subsided, and he sat down again.

"You are too clever for me, M. Poirot. Yes, it was Lily we quarrelled about. Reuben had his knife into her; he had ferreted out something or other about the girl—false references, something of that kind. I don't believe a word of it myself.

"And then he went further than he had any right to go, talked about her stealing down at night and getting out of the house to meet some fellow or other. My God! I gave it to him; I told him that better men than he had been killed for saying less. That shut him up. Reuben was inclined to be a bit afraid of me when I got going."

"I hardly wonder at it," murmured Poirot politely.

"I think a lot of Lily Margrave," said Victor in another tone. "A nice girl through and through."

Poirot did not answer. He was staring in front of him, seemingly lost in abstraction. He came out of his brown study with a jerk.

"I must, I think, promenade myself a little. There is a hotel here, yes?"

"Two," said Victor Astwell, "the Golf Hotel up by the links and the Mitre down by the station."

"I thank you," said Poirot. "Yes, certainly I must promenade myself a little."

The Golf Hotel, as befits its name, stands on the golf links almost adjoining the club house. It was to this hostelry that Poirot repaired first in the course of that "promenade" which he had advertised himself as being about to take. The little man had his own way of doing things. Three minutes after he had entered the Golf Hotel he was in private consultation with Miss Langdon, the manageress.

"I regret to incommode you in any way, Mademoiselle," said Poirot, "but you see I am a detective."

Simplicity always appealed to him. In this case the method proved efficacious at once.

"A detective!" exclaimed Miss Langdon, looking at him doubtfully.

"Not from Scotland Yard," Poirot assured her. "In fact—you may have noticed it? I am not an Englishman. No, I make the private inquiries into the death of Sir Reuben Astwell."

"You don't say, now!" Miss Langdon goggled at him expectantly.

"Precisely," said Poirot beaming. "Only to

someone of discretion like yourself would I reveal the fact. I think, Mademoiselle, you may be able to aid me. Can you tell me of any gentleman staying here on the night of the murder who was absent from the hotel that evening and returned to it about twelve or half past?"

Miss Langdon's eyes opened wider than ever.

"You don't think—?" she breathed.

"That you had the murderer here? No, but I have reason to believe that a guest staying here promenaded himself in the direction of Mon Repos that night, and if so he may have seen something which, though conveying no meaning to him, might be very useful to me."

The manageress nodded her head sapiently, with an air of one thoroughly well up in the annals of detective logic.

"I understand perfectly. Now, let me see; who did we have staying here?"

She frowned, evidently running over the names in her mind, and helping her memory by occasionally checking them off on her finger-tips.

"Captain Swann, Mr. Elkins, Major Blyunt, old Mr. Benson. No, really, sir, I don't believe anyone went out that evening."

"You would have noticed if they had done so, eh?"

"Oh, yes, sir, it is not very usual, you see. I mean gentlemen go out to dinner and all that, but they don't go out after dinner, because—well, there is nowhere to go to, is there?"

The attractions of Abbots Cross were golf and nothing but golf.

"That is so," agreed Poirot. "Then, as far as you remember, Mademoiselle, nobody from here was out that night?"

"Captain England and his wife were out to dinner."

Poirot shook his head.

"That is not the kind of thing I mean. I will try the other hotel; the Mitre, is it not?"

"Oh, the Mitre," said Miss Langdon. "Of course, anyone might have gone out walking from *there*."

The disparagement of her tone, though vague, was evident, and Poirot beat a tactful retreat.

Ten minutes later he was repeating the scene, this time with Miss Cole, the brusque manageress of the Mitre, a less pretentious hotel with lower prices, situated close to the station.

"There was one gentleman out late that night, came in about half past twelve, as far as I can remember. Quite a habit of his it was, to go out for a walk at that time of the evening. He had done it once or twice before. Let me see now, what was his name? Just for the moment I can't remember it."

She pulled a large ledger towards her and began turning over the pages.

"Nineteenth, twentieth, twenty-first, twenty-second. Ah, here we are. Naylor, Captain Humphrey Naylor."

"He had stayed here before? You know him well?"

"Once before," said Miss Cole, "about a fortnight earlier. He went out then in the evening, I remember."

"He came to play golf, eh?"

"I suppose so," said Miss Cole, "that's what most of the gentlemen come for."

"Very true," said Poirot. "Well, Mademoiselle, I thank you infinitely, and I wish you good day."

He went back to Mon Repos with a very thoughtful face. Once or twice he drew something from his pocket and looked at it.

"It must be done," he murmured to himself, "and soon, as soon as I can make the opportunity."

His first proceeding on reentering the house was to ask Parsons where Miss Margrave might be found. He was told that she was in the small study dealing with Lady Astwell's correspondence, and the information seemed to afford Poirot satisfaction.

He found the little study without difficulty. Lily Margrave was seated at a desk by the window, writing. But for her the room was empty. Poirot carefully shut the door behind him and came towards the girl.

"I may have a little minute of your time, Mademoiselle, you will be so kind?"

"Certainly."

Lily Margrave put the papers aside and turned towards him.

"What can I do for you?"

"On the evening of the tragedy, Mademoiselle, I understand that when Lady Astwell went to her husband you went straight up to bed. Is that so?"

Lily Margrave nodded.

"You did not come down again, by any chance?"

The girl shook her head.

"I think you said, Mademoiselle, that you had not at any time that evening been in the Tower room?"

"I don't remember saying so, but as a matter of fact that is quite true. I was not in the Tower room that evening."

Poirot raised his eyebrows.

"Curious," he murmured.

"What do you mean?"

"Very curious," murmured Hercule Poirot again. "How do you account, then, for this?"

He drew from his pocket a little scrap of stained green chiffon and held it up for the girl's inspection.

Her expression did not change, but he felt rather than heard the sharp intake of breath.

"I don't understand, M. Poirot."

"You wore, I understand, a green chiffon dress that evening, Mademoiselle. This—" he tapped the scrap in his fingers—"was torn from it."

"And you found it in the Tower room?" asked the girl sharply. "Whereabouts?"

Hercule Poirot looked at the ceiling.

"For the moment shall we just say—in the Tower room?"

For the first time, a look of fear sprang into the girl's eyes. She began to speak, then checked herself. Poirot watched her small white hands clenching themselves on the edge of the desk.

"I wonder if I did go into the Tower room that evening?" she mused. "Before dinner, I mean. I don't think so. I am almost sure I didn't. If that scrap has been in the Tower room all this time, it seems to me a very extraordinary thing the police did not find it right away."

"The police," said the little man, "do not think of things that Hercule Poirot thinks of."

"I may have run in there for a minute just before dinner," mused Lily Margrave, "or it may have been the night before. I wore the same dress then. Yes, I am almost sure it was the night before."

"I think not," said Poirot evenly.

"Why?"

He only shook his head slowly from side to side.

"What do you mean?" whispered the girl.

She was leaning forward, staring at him, all the colour ebbing out of her face.

"You do not notice, Mademoiselle, that this fragment is stained? There is no doubt about it, that stain is human blood."

"You mean—"

"I mean, Mademoiselle, that you were in the Tower room *after* the crime was committed, not before. I think you will do well to tell me the whole truth, lest worse should befall you."

He stood up now, a stern little figure of a man, his forefinger pointed accusingly at the girl.

"How did you find out?" gasped Lily.

"No matter, Mademoiselle. I tell you Hercule Poirot *knows*. I know all about Captain Humphrey Naylor, and that you went down to meet him that night."

Lily suddenly put her head down on her arms and burst into tears. Immediately Poirot relinquished his accusing attitude.

"There, there, my little one," he said, patting the girl on the shoulder. "Do not distress yourself. Impossible to deceive Hercule Poirot; once realize that and all your troubles will be at an end. And now you will tell me the whole story, will you not? You will tell old Papa Poirot?"

"It is not what you think, it isn't, indeed. Humphrey—my brother—never touched a hair of his head."

"Your brother, eh?" said Poirot. "So that is how

61

the land lies. Well, if you wish to save him from suspicion, you must tell me the whole story now, without reservation."

Lily sat up again, pushing back the hair from her forehead. After a minute or two, she began to speak in a low, clear voice.

"I will tell you the truth, M. Poirot. I can see now that it would be absurd to do anything else. My real name is Lily Naylor, and Humphrey is my only brother. Some years ago, when he was out in Africa, he discovered a gold mine, or rather, I should say, discovered the presence of gold. I can't tell you this part of it properly, because I don't understand the technical details, but what it amounted to was this:

"The thing seemed likely to be a very big undertaking, and Humphrey came home with letters to Sir Reuben Astwell in the hopes of getting him interested in the matter. I don't understand the rights of it even now, but I gather that Sir Reuben sent out an expert to report, and that he subsequently told my brother that the expert's report was unfavourable and that he, Humphrey, had made a great mistake. My brother went back to Africa on an expedition into the interior and was lost sight of. It was assumed that he and the expedition had perished.

"It was soon after that that a company was formed to exploit the Mpala Gold Fields. When my brother got back to England he at once jumped to the conclusion that these gold fields were identical with those he had discovered. Sir Reuben Astwell had apparently nothing to do with this company, and they had seemingly discovered the place on their own. But my brother was not satisfied; he was convinced that Sir Reuben had deliberately swindled him.

"He became more and more violent and unhappy about the matter. We two are alone in the world, M. Poirot, and as it was necessary then for me to go out and earn my own living, I conceived the idea of taking a post in this household and trying to find out if any connection existed between Sir Reuben and the Mpala Gold Fields. For obvious reasons I concealed my real name, and I'll admit frankly that I used a forged reference.

"There were many applicants for the post, most of them with better qualifications than mine, so— well, M. Poirot, I wrote a beautiful letter from the Duchess of Perthshire, who I knew had gone to America. I thought a duchess would have a great effect upon Lady Astwell, and I was quite right. She engaged me on the spot.

"Since then I have been that hateful thing, a spy, and until lately with no success. Sir Reuben is not a man to give away his business secrets, but when Victor Astwell came back from Africa he was less guarded in his talk, and I began to believe that, after all, Humphrey had not been mistaken. My brother came down here about a fortnight before the murder, and I crept out of the house to meet him secretly at night. I told him the things Victor Astwell had said, and he became very excited and assured me I was definitely on the right track.

"But after that things began to go wrong; someone must have seen me stealing out of the house and have reported the matter to Sir Reuben. He became suspicious and hunted up my references, and soon discovered the fact that they were forged. The crisis came on the day of the murder. I think he thought I was after his wife's jewels. Whatever his suspicions were, he had no intention of allowing me to remain any longer at Mon Repos, though he agreed not to prosecute me on account of the references. Lady Astwell took my part throughout and stood up valiantly to Sir Reuben."

She paused. Poirot's face was very grave.

"And now, Mademoiselle," he said, "we come to the night of the murder."

Lily swallowed hard and nodded her head.

"To begin with, M. Poirot, I must tell you that my brother had come down again, and that I had arranged to creep out and meet him once more. I went up to my room, as I have said, but I did not go to bed. Instead, I waited till I thought everyone was asleep, and then stole downstairs again and out by the side door. I met Humphrey and acquainted him in a few hurried words with what had occurred. I told him that I believed the papers he wanted were in Sir Reuben's safe in the Tower room, and we agreed as a last desperate adventure to try and get hold of them that night.

"I was to go in first and see that the way was clear. I heard the church clock strike twelve as I went in by the side door. I was half-way up the stairs leading to the Tower room, when I heard a thud of something falling, and a voice cried out, 'My God!' A minute or two afterwards the door of the Tower room opened, and Charles Leverson came out. I could see his face quite clearly in the moonlight, but I was crouching some way below him on the stairs where it was dark, and he did not see me at all.

"He stood there a moment swaying on his feet and looking ghastly. He seemed to be listening; then with an effort he seemed to pull himself together and, opening the door into the Tower room, called out something about there being no harm done. His voice was quite jaunty and debonair, but his face gave the lie to it. He waited a minute more, and then slowly went on upstairs and out of sight.

"When he had gone I waited a minute or two and then crept to the Tower room door. I had a feeling that something tragic had happened. The main light was out, but the desk lamp was on, and by its light I saw Sir Reuben lying on the floor by the desk. I don't know how I managed it, but I nerved myself at last to go over and kneel down by him. I saw at once that he was dead, struck down from behind, and also that he couldn't have been dead long; I touched his hand and it was still quite warm. It was just horrible, M. Poirot. Horrible!"

She shuddered again at the remembrance.

"And then?" said Poirot, looking at her keenly.

Lily Margrave nodded.

"Yes, M. Poirot, I know what you are thinking. Why didn't I give the alarm and raise the house? I should have done so, I know, but it came over me in a flash, as I knelt there, that my quarrel with Sir Reuben, my stealing out to meet Humphrey, the fact that I was being sent away on the morrow, made a fatal sequence. They would say that I had let Humphrey in, and that Humphrey had killed Sir Reuben out of revenge. If I said that I had seen Charles Leverson leaving the room, no one would believe me.

"It was terrible, M. Poirot! I knelt there, and thought and thought, and the more I thought the more my nerve failed me. Presently I noticed Sir Reuben's keys which had dropped from his pocket as he fell. Among them was the key of the safe, the combination word I already knew, since Lady Astwell had mentioned it once in my hearing. I went over to that safe, M. Poirot, unlocked it and rummaged through the papers I found there.

"In the end I found what I was looking for.

Humphrey had been perfectly right. Sir Reuben was behind the Mpala Gold Fields, and he had deliberately swindled Humphrey. That made it all the worse. It gave a perfectly definite motive for Humphrey having committed the crime. I put the papers back in the safe, left the key in the door of it, and went straight upstairs to my room. In the morning I pretended to be surprised and horror-stricken, like everyone else, when the housemaid discovered the body."

She stopped and looked piteously across at Poirot.

"You do believe me, M. Poirot. Oh, do say you believe me!"

"I believe you, Mademoiselle," said Poirot; "you have explained many things that puzzled me. Your absolute certainty, for one thing, that Charles Leverson had committed the crime, and at the same time your persistent efforts to keep me from coming down here."

Lily nodded.

"I was afraid of you," she admitted frankly. "Lady Astwell could not know, as I did, that Charles was guilty, and I couldn't say anything. I hoped against hope that you would refuse to take the case."

"But for that obvious anxiety on your part, I might have done so," said Poirot drily.

Lily looked at him swiftly, her lips trembled a little.

"And now, M. Poirot, what—what are you going to do?"

"As far as you are concerned, Mademoiselle, nothing. I believe your story, and I accept it. The next step is to go to London and see Inspector Miller."

"And then?" asked Lily.

"And then," said Poirot, "we shall see."

Outside the door of the study he looked once more at the little square of stained green chiffon which he held in his hand.

"Amazing," he murmured to himself complacently, "the ingenuity of Hercule Poirot."

Detective-Inspector Miller was not particularly fond of M. Hercule Poirot. He did not belong to that small band of inspectors at the Yard who welcomed the little Belgian's cooperation. He was wont to say that Hercule Poirot was much overrated. In this case he felt pretty sure of himself, and greeted Poirot with high good humour in consequence.

"Acting for Lady Astwell, are you? Well, you have taken up a mare's nest in that case."

"There is, then, no possible doubt about the matter?"

Miller winked. "Never was a clearer case, short of catching a murderer absolutely red-handed."

"M. Leverson has made a statement, I understand?"

"He had better have kept his mouth shut," said the detective. "He repeats over and over again that he went straight up to his room and never went near his uncle. That's a fool story on the face of it."

"It is certainly against the weight of evidence," murmured Poirot. "How does he strike you, this young M. Leverson?"

"Darned young fool."

"A weak character, eh?"

The inspector nodded.

"One would hardly think a young man of that type would have the—how do you say it—the bowels to commit such a crime."

"On the face of it, no," agreed the inspector. "But, bless you, I have come across the same thing many times. Get a weak, dissipated young man into a corner, fill him up with a drop too much to drink, and for a limited amount of time you can turn him into a fire-eater. A weak man in a corner is more dangerous than a strong man."

"That is true, yes; that is true what you say."

Miller unbent a little further.

"Of course, it is all right for you, M. Poirot," he said. "You get your fees just the same, and naturally you have to make a pretence of examining the evidence to satisfy her ladyship. I can understand all that."

"You understand such interesting things," murmured Poirot, and took his leave.

His next call was upon the solicitor representing Charles Leverson. Mr. Mayhew was a thin, dry, cautious gentleman. He received Poirot with reserve. Poirot, however, had his own ways of inducing confidence. In ten minutes' time the two were talking together amicably.

"You will understand," said Poirot, "I am acting in this case solely on behalf of Mr. Leverson. That is Lady Astwell's wish. She is convinced that he is not guilty."

"Yes, yes, quite so," said Mr. Mayhew without enthusiasm.

Poirot's eyes twinkled. "You do not perhaps attach much importance to the opinions of Lady Astwell?" he suggested.

"She might be just as sure of his guilt tomorrow," said the lawyer drily.

"Her intuitions are not evidence certainly," agreed Poirot, "and on the face of it the case looks very black against this poor young man."

"It is a pity he said what he did to the police," said the lawyer; "it will be no good his sticking to that story."

"Has he stuck to it with you?" inquired Poirot.

Mayhew nodded. "It never varies an iota. He repeats it like a parrot."

"And that is what destroys your faith in him," mused the other. "Ah, don't deny it," he added quickly, holding up an arresting hand. "I see it only too plainly. In your heart you believe him guilty. But listen now to me, to me, Hercule Poirot. I present to you a case.

"This young man comes home, he has drunk the cocktail, the cocktail, and again the cocktail, also without doubt the English whisky and soda many times. He is full of, what you call it? the courage Dutch, and in that mood he let himself into the house with his latchkey, and he goes with unsteady steps up to the Tower room. He looks in at the door and sees in the dim light his uncle, apparently bending over the desk.

"M. Leverson is full, as we have said, of the courage Dutch. He lets himself go, he tells his uncle just what he thinks of him. He defies him, he insults him, and the more his uncle does not answer back, the more he is encouraged to go on, to repeat himself, to say the same thing over and over again, and each time more loudly. But at last the continued silence of his uncle awakens an apprehension. He goes nearer to him, he lays his hand on his uncle's shoulder, and his uncle's figure crumples under his touch and sinks in a heap to the ground.

"He is sobered then, this M. Leverson. The chair falls with a crash, and he bends over Sir Reuben. He realizes what has happened, he looks at his hand covered with something warm and red. He is in a panic then, he would give anything on earth to recall the cry which has just sprung from his lips, echoing through the house.

Mechanically he picks up the chair, then he hastens out through the door and listens. He fancies he hears a sound, and immediately, automatically, he pretends to be speaking to his uncle through the open door.

"The sound is not repeated. He is convinced he has been mistaken in thinking he heard one. Now all is silence, he creeps up to his room, and at once it occurs to him how much better it will be if he pretends never to have been near his uncle that night. So he tells his story. Parsons at that time, remember, has said nothing of what he heard. When he does do so, it is too late for M. Leverson to change. He is stupid, and he is obstinate, he sticks to his story. Tell me, Monsieur, is that not possible?"

"Yes," said the lawyer, "I suppose in the way you put it that it is possible."

Poirot rose to his feet.

"You have the privilege of seeing M. Leverson," he said. "Put to him the story I have told you, and ask him if it is not true."

Outside the lawyer's office, Poirot hailed a taxi.

"Three-four-eight Harley Street," he murmured to the driver.

Poirot's departure for London had taken Lady Astwell by surprise, for the little man had not made any mention of what he proposed doing. On his return, after an absence of twenty-four hours, he was informed by Parsons that Lady Astwell would like to see him as soon as possible. Poirot found the lady in her own boudoir. She was lying down on the divan, her head propped up by cushions, and she looked startlingly ill and haggard; far more so than she had done on the day Poirot arrived.

"So you have come back, M. Poirot?"

"I have returned, Madame."

"You went to London?"

Poirot nodded.

"You didn't tell me you were going," said Lady Astwell sharply.

"A thousand apologies, Madame, I am in error, I should have done so. *La prochaine fois*—"

"You will do exactly the same," interrupted Lady Astwell with a shrewd touch of humour. "Do things first and tell people afterwards, that is your motto right enough."

"Perhaps it has also been Madame's motto?" His eyes twinkled.

"Now and then, perhaps," admitted the other. "What did you go up to London for, M. Poirot? You can tell me now, I suppose?"

"I had an interview with the good Inspector Miller, and also with the excellent Mr. Mayhew."

Lady Astwell's eyes searched his face.

"And you think, now—?" she said slowly.

Poirot's eyes were fixed on her steadily.

"That there is a possibility of Charles Leverson's innocence," he said gravely.

"Ah!" Lady Astwell half-sprung up, sending two cushions rolling to the ground. "I was right, then, I was right!"

"I said a possibility, Madame, that is all."

Something in his tone seemed to strike her. She raised herself on one elbow and regarded him piercingly.

"Can I do anything?" she asked.

"Yes," he nodded his head, "you can tell me, Lady Astwell, why you suspect Owen Trefusis."

"I have told you I *know*—that's all."

"Unfortunately, that is not enough," said Poirot drily. "Cast your mind back to the fatal evening, Madame. Remember each detail, each tiny happening. What did you notice or observe about the secretary? I, Hercule Poirot, tell you there must have been *something*."

Lady Astwell shook her head.

"I hardly noticed him at all that evening," she said, "and I certainly was not thinking of him."

"Your mind was taken up by something else?"

"Yes."

"With your husband's animus against Miss Lily Margrave?"

"That's right," said Lady Astwell, nodding her head; "you seem to know all about it, M. Poirot."

"Me, I know everything," declared the little man with an absurdly grandiose air.

"I am fond of Lily, M. Poirot; you have seen that for yourself. Reuben began kicking up a rumpus about some reference or other of hers. Mind you, I don't say she hadn't cheated about it. She had. But, bless you, I have done many worse things than that in the old days. You have got to be up to all sorts of tricks to get round theatrical managers. There is nothing I wouldn't have written, or said, or done, in my time.

"Lily wanted this job, and she put in a lot of slick work that was not quite—well, quite the thing, you know. Men are so stupid about that sort of thing; Lily really might have been a bank clerk absconding with millions for the fuss he made about it. I was terribly worried all the evening, because, although I could usually get round Reuben in the end, he was terribly pigheaded at times, poor darling. So of course I hadn't time to go noticing secretaries, not that one does notice Mr. Trefusis much, anyway. He is just there and that's all there is to it."

"I have noticed that fact about M. Trefusis," said Poirot. "His is not a personality that stands forth, that shines, that hits you cr-r-rack."

"No," said Lady Astwell, "he is not like Victor."

"M. Victor Astwell is, I should say, explosive."

"That is a splendid word for him," said Lady Astwell. "He explodes all over the house, like

75

one of those thingimyjig firework things."

"A somewhat quick temper, I should imagine?" suggested Poirot.

"Oh, he's a perfect devil when roused," said Lady Astwell, "but bless you, *I'm* not afraid of him. All bark and no bite to Victor."

Poirot looked at the ceiling.

"And you can tell me nothing about the secretary that evening?" he murmured gently.

"I tell you, M. Poirot, I *know.* It's intuition. A woman's intuition—"

"Will not hang a man," said Poirot, "and what is more to the point, it will not save a man from being hanged. Lady Astwell, if you sincerely believe that M. Leverson is innocent, and that your suspicions of the secretary are well-founded, will you consent to a little experiment?"

"What kind of an experiment?" demanded Lady Astwell suspiciously.

"Will you permit yourself to be put into a condition of hypnosis?"

"Whatever for?"

Poirot leaned forward.

"If I were to tell you, Madame, that your intuition is based on certain facts recorded subconsciously, you would probably be sceptical. I will only say, then, that this experiment I propose may be of great importance to that unfortunate young man, Charles Leverson. You will not refuse?"

"Who is going to put me into a trance?" demanded Lady Astwell suspiciously. "You?"

"A friend of mine, Lady Astwell, arrives, if I mistake not, at this very minute. I hear the wheels of the car outside."

"Who is he?"

"A Dr. Cazalet of Harley Street."

"Is he—all right?" asked Lady Astwell apprehensively.

"He is not a quack, Madame, if that is what you mean. You can trust yourself in his hands quite safely."

"Well," said Lady Astwell with a sigh, "I think it is all bunkum, but you can try if you like. Nobody is going to say that I stood in your way."

"A thousand thanks, Madame."

Poirot hurried from the room. In a few minutes he returned ushering in a cheerful, round-faced little man, with spectacles, who was very upsetting to Lady Astwell's conception of what a hypnotist should look like. Poirot introduced them.

"Well," said Lady Astwell good-humouredly, "how do we start this tomfoolery?"

"Quite simple, Lady Astwell, quite simple," said the little doctor. "Just lean back, so—that's right, that's right. No need to be uneasy."

"I am not in the least uneasy," said Lady Astwell. "I should like to see anyone hypnotizing me against my will."

Dr. Cazalet smiled broadly.

"Yes, but if you consent, it won't be against your will, will it?" he said cheerfully. "That's right. Turn off that other light, will you, M. Poirot? Just let yourself go to sleep, Lady Astwell."

He shifted his position a little.

"It's getting late. You are sleepy—very sleepy. Your eyelids are heavy, they are closing—closing—closing. Soon you will be asleep. . . ."

His voice droned on, low, soothing, and monotonous. Presently he leaned forward and gently lifted Lady Astwell's right eyelid. Then he turned to Poirot, nodding in a satisfied manner.

"That's all right," he said in a low voice. "Shall I go ahead?"

"If you please."

The doctor spoke out sharply and authoritatively: "You are asleep, Lady Astwell, but you hear me, and you can answer my questions."

Without stirring or raising an eyelid, the motionless figure on the sofa replied in a low, monotonous voice:

"I hear you. I can answer your questions."

"Lady Astwell, I want you to go back to the evening on which your husband was murdered. You remember that evening?"

"Yes."

"You are at the dinner table. Describe to me what you saw and felt."

The prone figure stirred a little restlessly.

"I am in great distress. I am worried about Lily."

"We know that; tell us what you saw."

"Victor is eating all the salted almonds; he is greedy. Tomorrow I shall tell Parsons not to put the dish on that side of the table."

"Go on, Lady Astwell."

"Reuben is in a bad humour tonight. I don't think it is altogether about Lily. It is something to do with business. Victor looks at him in a queer way."

"Tell us about Mr. Trefusis, Lady Astwell."

"His left shirt cuff is frayed. He puts a lot of grease on his hair. I wish men didn't, it ruins the covers in the drawing room."

Cazalet looked at Poirot; the other made a motion with his head.

"It is after dinner, Lady Astwell, you are having coffee. Describe the scene to me."

"The coffee is good tonight. It varies. Cook is very unreliable over her coffee. Lily keeps looking out of the window, I don't know why. Now Reuben comes into the room; he is in one of his worst moods tonight, and bursts out with a perfect flood of abuse to poor Mr. Trefusis. Mr. Trefusis has his hand round the paper knife, the big one with the sharp blade like a knife. How hard he is grasping it; his knuckles are quite white. Look, he has dug it so hard in the table that the point snaps. He holds it just as you would hold a dagger you were going to stick into someone. There, they have gone out together now. Lily has got her green evening dress on; she looks so pretty in green, just like a lily. I must have the covers cleaned next week."

"Just a minute, Lady Astwell."

The doctor leaned across to Poirot.

"We have got it, I think," he murmured; "that action with the paper knife, that's what convinced her that the secretary did the thing."

"Let us go on to the Tower room now."

The doctor nodded, and began once more to question Lady Astwell in his high, decisive voice.

"It is later in the evening; you are in the Tower room with your husband. You and he have had a terrible scene together, have you not?"

Again the figure stirred uneasily.

"Yes—terrible—terrible. We said dreadful things—both of us."

"Never mind that now. You can see the room clearly, the curtains were drawn, the lights were on."

"Not the middle light, only the desk light."

"You are leaving your husband now, you are saying good night to him."

"No, I was too angry."

"It is the last time you will see him; very soon he will be murdered. Do you know who murdered him, Lady Astwell?"

"Yes. Mr. Trefusis."

"Why do you say that?"

"Because of the bulge—the bulge in the curtain."

"There was a bulge in the curtain?"

"Yes."

"You saw it?"

"Yes. I almost touched it."

"Was there a man concealed there—Mr. Trefusis?"

"Yes."

"How do you know?"

For the first time the monotonous answering voice hesitated and lost confidence.

"I—I—because of the paper knife."

Poirot and the doctor again interchanged swift glances.

"I don't understand you, Lady Astwell. There was a bulge in the curtain, you say? Someone concealed there? You didn't see that person?"

"No."

"You thought it was Mr. Trefusis because of the way he held the paper knife earlier?"

"Yes."

"But Mr. Trefusis had gone to bed, had he not?"

"Yes—yes, that's right, he had gone away to his room."

"So he couldn't have been behind the curtain in the window?"

"No—no, of course not, he wasn't there."

"He had said good night to your husband some time before, hadn't he?"

"Yes."

"And you didn't see him again?"

"No."

She was stirring now, throwing herself about, moaning faintly.

"She is coming out," said the doctor. "Well, I think we have got all we can, eh?"

Poirot nodded. The doctor leaned over Lady Astwell.

"You are waking," he murmured softly. "You are waking now. In another minute you will open your eyes."

The two men waited, and presently Lady Astwell sat upright and stared at them both.

"Have I been having a nap?"

"That's it, Lady Astwell, just a little sleep," said the doctor.

She looked at him.

"Some of your hocus-pocus, eh?"

"You don't feel any the worse, I hope," he asked.

Lady Astwell yawned.

"I feel rather tired and done up."

The doctor rose.

"I will ask them to send you up some coffee," he said, "and we will leave you for the present."

"Did I—say anything?" Lady Astwell called after them as they reached the door.

Poirot smiled back at her.

"Nothing of great importance, Madame. You informed us that the drawing room covers needed cleaning."

"So they do," said Lady Astwell. "You needn't have put me into a trance to get me to tell you that." She laughed good-humouredly. "Anything more?"

"Do you remember M. Trefusis picking up a paper knife in the drawing room that night?" asked Poirot.

"I don't know, I'm sure," said Lady Astwell. "He may have done so."

"Does a bulge in the curtain convey anything to you?"

Lady Astwell frowned.

"I seem to remember," she said slowly. "No— it's gone, and yet—"

"Do not distress yourself, Lady Astwell," said Poirot quickly; "it is of no importance—of no importance whatever."

The doctor went with Poirot to the latter's room.

"Well," said Cazalet, "I think this explains things pretty clearly. No doubt when Sir Reuben was dressing down the secretary, the latter grabbed tight hold on a paper knife, and had to exercise a good deal of self-control to prevent himself answering back. Lady Astwell's conscious mind was wholly taken up with the problem of Lily

Margrave, but her subconscious mind noticed and misconstrued the action.

"It implanted in her the firm conviction that Trefusis murdered Sir Reuben. Now we come to the bulge in the curtain. That is interesting. I take it from what you have told me of the Tower room that the desk was right in the window. There are curtains across that window, of course?"

"Yes, *mon ami*, black velvet curtains."

"And there is room in the embrasure of the window for anyone to remain concealed behind them?"

"There would be just room, I think."

"Then there seems at least a possibility," said the doctor slowly, "that someone was concealed in the room, but if so it could not be the secretary, since they both saw him leave the room. It could not be Victor Astwell, for Trefusis met him going out, and it could not be Lily Margrave. Whoever it was must have been concealed there *before* Sir Reuben entered the room that evening. You have told me pretty well how the land lies. Now what about Captain Naylor? Could it have been he who was concealed there?"

"It is always possible," admitted Poirot. "He certainly dined at the hotel, but how soon he went out afterwards is difficult to fix exactly. He returned about half past twelve."

"Then it might have been he," said the doctor, "and if so, he committed the crime. He had the motive, and there was a weapon near at hand. You don't seem satisfied with the idea, though?"

"Me, I have other ideas," confessed Poirot. "Tell me now, *M. le Docteur*, supposing for one minute that Lady Astwell herself had committed this crime, would she necessarily betray the fact in the hypnotic state?"

The doctor whistled.

"So that's what you are getting at? Lady Astwell is the criminal, eh? Of course—it is possible; I never thought of it till this minute. She was the last to be with him, and no one saw him alive afterwards. As to your question, I should be inclined to say—no. Lady Astwell would go into the hypnotic state with a strong mental reservation to say nothing of her own part in the crime. She would answer my questions truthfully, but she would be dumb on that one point. Yet I should hardly have expected her to be so insistent on Mr. Trefusis's guilt."

"I comprehend," said Poirot. "But I have not said that I believe Lady Astwell to be the criminal. It is a suggestion, that is all."

"It is an interesting case," said the doctor after a minute or two. "Granting Charles Leverson is innocent, there are so many possibilities, Humphrey Naylor, Lady Astwell, and even Lily Margrave."

"There is another you have not mentioned," said Poirot quietly, "Victor Astwell. According to his own story, he sat in his room with the door open waiting for Charles Leverson's return, but we have only his own words for it, you comprehend?"

"He is the bad-tempered fellow, isn't he?" asked the doctor. "The one you told me about?"

"That is so," agreed Poirot.

The doctor rose to his feet.

"Well, I must be getting back to town. You will let me know how things shape, won't you?"

After the doctor had left, Poirot pulled the bell for George.

"A cup of *tisane*, George. My nerves are much disturbed."

"Certainly, sir," said George. "I will prepare it immediately."

Ten minutes later he brought a steaming cup to his master. Poirot inhaled the noxious fumes with pleasure. As he sipped it, he soliloquized aloud.

"The chase is different all over the world. To catch the fox you ride hard with the dogs. You shout, you run, it is a matter of speed. I have not shot the stag myself, but I understand that to do so you crawl for many long, long hours upon your stomach. My friend Hastings has recounted the affair to me. Our method here, my good George, must be neither of these. Let us reflect upon the household cat. For many long, weary hours, he watches the mousehole, he makes no movement, he betrays no energy, but—he does not go away."

He sighed and put the empty cup down on its saucer.

"I told you to pack for a few days. Tomorrow, my good George, you will go to London and bring down what is necessary for a fortnight."

"Very good, sir," said George. As usual he displayed no emotion.

The apparently permanent presence of Hercule Poirot at Mon Repos was disquieting to many people. Victor Astwell remonstrated with his sister-in-law about it.

"It's all very well, Nancy. You don't know what fellows of that kind are like. He has found jolly comfortable quarters here, and he is evidently going to settle down comfortably for about a month, charging you several guineas a day all the while."

Lady Astwell's reply was to the effect that she could manage her own affairs without inter-ference.

Lily Margrave tried earnestly to conceal her perturbation. At the time, she had felt sure that Poirot believed her story. Now she was not so certain.

Poirot did not play an entirely quiescent game. On the fifth day of his sojourn he brought down a small thumbograph album to dinner. As a method of getting the thumbprints of the household, it seemed a rather clumsy device, yet not perhaps so clumsy as it seemed, since no one could afford to refuse their thumbprints. Only after the little man had retired to bed did Victor Astwell state his views.

"You see what it means, Nancy. He is out after one of us."

"Don't be absurd, Victor."

"Well, what other meaning could that blinking little book of his have?"

"M. Poirot knows what he is doing," said Lady Astwell complacently, and looked with some meaning at Owen Trefusis.

On another occasion, Poirot introduced the game of tracing footprints on a sheet of paper. The following morning, going with his soft cat-like tread into the library, the detective startled Owen Trefusis, who leaped from his chair as though he had been shot.

"You must really excuse me, M. Poirot," he said primly, "but you have us on the jump."

"Indeed, how is that?" demanded the little man innocently.

"I will admit," said the secretary, "that I thought the case against Charles Leverson utterly over-whelming. You apparently do not find it so."

Poirot was standing looking out of the window. He turned suddenly to the other.

"I shall tell you something, M. Trefusis—in confidence."

"Yes?"

Poirot seemed in no hurry to begin. He waited a minute, hesitating. When he did speak, the opening words were coincident with the opening and shutting of the front door. For a man saying something in confidence, he spoke rather loudly, his voice drowning the sound of a footstep in the hall outside.

"I shall tell you this in confidence, Mr. Trefusis. There is new evidence. It goes to prove that when Charles Leverson entered the Tower room that night, Sir Reuben was already dead."

The secretary stared at him.

"But what evidence? Why have we not heard of it?"

"You *will* hear," said the little man mysteriously. "In the meantime, you and I alone know the secret."

He skipped nimbly out of the room, and almost collided with Victor Astwell in the hall outside.

"You have just come in, eh, monsieur?"

Astwell nodded.

"Beastly day outside," he said breathing hard, "cold and blowy."

"Ah," said Poirot, "I shall not promenade myself today—me, I am like a cat, I sit by the fire and keep myself warm."

"*Ça marche*, George," Poirot said that evening to the faithful valet, rubbing his hands as he spoke, "they are on the tenterhooks—the jump! It is hard,

George, to play the game of the cat, the waiting game, but it answers, yes, it answers wonderfully. Tomorrow we make a further effect."

On the following day, Trefusis was obliged to go up to town. He went up by the same train as Victor Astwell. No sooner had they left the house than Poirot was galvanized into a fever of activity.

"Come, George, let us hurry to work. If the housemaid should approach these rooms, you must delay her. Speak to her sweet nothings, George, and keep her in the corridor."

He went first to the secretary's room, and began a thorough search. Not a drawer or a shelf was left uninspected. Then he replaced everything hurriedly, and declared his quest finished. George, on guard in the doorway, gave way to a deferential cough.

"If you will excuse me, sir?"

"Yes, my good George?"

"The shoes, sir. The two pairs of brown shoes were on the second shelf, and the patent leather ones were on the shelf underneath. In replacing them you have reversed the order."

"Marvellous!" cried Poirot, holding up his hands. "But let us not distress ourselves over that. It is of no importance, I assure you, George. Never will M. Trefusis notice such a trifling matter."

"As you think, sir," said George.

"It is your business to notice such things," said Poirot encouragingly as he clapped the other on the shoulder. "It reflects credit upon you."

The valet did not reply, and when, later in the day, the proceeding was repeated in the room of Victor Astwell, he made no comment on the fact that Mr. Astwell's underclothing was not returned to its drawers strictly according to plan. Yet, in the second case at least, events proved the valet to be right and Poirot wrong. Victor Astwell came storming into the drawing room that evening.

"Now, look here, you blasted little Belgian jackanapes, what do you mean by searching my room? What the devil do you think you are going to find there? I won't have it, do you hear? That's what comes of having a ferreting little spy in the house."

Poirot's hands spread themselves out eloquently as his words tumbled one over the other. He offered a hundred apologies, a thousand, a million. He had been maladroit, officious, he was confused. He had taken an unwarranted liberty. In the end the infuriated gentleman was forced to subside, still growling.

And again that evening, sipping his *tisane*, Poirot murmured to George:

"It marches, my good George, yes—it marches."

"Friday," observed Hercule Poirot thoughtfully, "is my lucky day."

"Indeed, sir."

"You are not superstitious, perhaps, my good George?"

"I prefer not to sit down thirteen at table, sir, and I am adverse to passing under ladders. I have no superstitions about a Friday, sir."

"That is well," said Poirot, "for, see you, today we make our Waterloo."

"Really, sir."

"You have such enthusiasm, my good George, you do not even ask what I propose to do."

"And what is that, sir?"

"Today, George, I make a final thorough search of the Tower room."

True enough, after breakfast, Poirot, with the permission of Lady Astwell, went to the scene of the crime. There, at various times of the morning, members of the household saw him crawling about on all fours, examining minutely the black velvet curtains and standing on high chairs to examine the picture frames on the wall. Lady Astwell for the first time displayed uneasiness.

"I have to admit it," she said. "He is getting on my nerves at last. He has something up his sleeve, and I don't know what it is. And the way he is crawling about on the floor up there like a dog makes me downright shivery. What is he looking for, I'd like to know? Lily, my dear, I wish you would go up and see what he is up to now. No, on the whole, I'd rather you stayed with me."

"Shall I go, Lady Astwell?" asked the secretary, rising from the desk.

"If you would, Mr. Trefusis."

Owen Trefusis left the room and mounted the stairs to the Tower room. At first glance, he thought the room was empty, there was certainly no sign of Hercule Poirot there. He was just returning to go down again when a sound caught his ears; he then saw the little man halfway down the spiral staircase that led to the bedroom above.

He was on his hands and knees; in his left hand was a little pocket lens, and through this he was examining minutely something on the woodwork beside the stair carpet.

As the secretary watched him, he uttered a sudden grunt, and slipped the lens into his pocket. He then rose to his feet, holding something between his finger and thumb. At that moment he became aware of the secretary's presence.

"Ah, hah! M. Trefusis, I didn't hear you enter."

He was in that moment a different man. Triumph and exultation beamed all over his face. Trefusis stared at him in surprise.

"What is the matter, M. Poirot? You look very pleased."

The little man puffed out his chest.

"Yes, indeed. See you I have at last found that which I have been looking for from the beginning. I have here between my finger and thumb the one thing necessary to convict the criminal."

"Then," the secretary raised his eyebrows, "it was not Charles Leverson?"

"It was not Charles Leverson," said Poirot. "Until this moment, though I know the criminal, I am not sure of his name, but at last all is clear."

He stepped down the stairs and tapped the secretary on the shoulder.

"I am obliged to go to London immediately. Speak to Lady Astwell for me. Will you request of her that everyone should be assembled in the Tower room this evening at nine o'clock? I shall be there then, and I shall reveal the truth. Ah, me, but I am well content."

And breaking into a fantastic little dance, he skipped from the Tower room. Trefusis was left staring after him.

A few minutes later Poirot appeared in the library, demanding if anyone could supply him with a little cardboard box.

"Unfortunately, I have not such a thing with me," he explained, "and there is something of great value that it is necessary for me to put inside."

From one of the drawers in the desk Trefusis produced a small box, and Poirot professed himself highly delighted with it.

He hurried upstairs with his treasure trove; meeting George on the landing, he handed the box to him.

"There is something of great importance inside," he explained. "Place it, my good George, in the second drawer of my dressing table, beside the jewel case that contains my pearl studs."

"Very good, sir," said George.

"Do not break it," said Poirot. "Be very careful. Inside that box is something that will hang a criminal."

"You don't say, sir," said George.

Poirot hurried down the stairs again and, seizing his hat, departed from the house at a brisk run.

His return was more unostentatious. The faithful George, according to orders, admitted him by the side door.

"They are all in the Tower room?" inquired Poirot.

"Yes, sir."

There was a murmured interchange of a few words, and then Poirot mounted with the triumphant step of the victor to that room where the murder had taken place less than a month ago. His eyes swept around the room. They were all there, Lady Astwell, Victor Astwell, Lily Margrave, the secretary, and Parsons, the butler. The latter was hovering by the door uncertainly.

"George, sir, said I should be needed here," said Parsons as Poirot made his appearance. "I don't know if that is right, sir?"

"Quite right," said Poirot. "Remain, I pray of you."

He advanced to the middle of the room.

"This has been a case of great interest," he said in a slow, reflective voice. "It is interesting because anyone might have murdered Sir Reuben Astwell. Who inherits his money? Charles Leverson and Lady Astwell. Who was with him last that night? Lady Astwell. Who quarrelled with him violently? Again Lady Astwell."

"What are you talking about?" cried Lady Astwell. "I don't understand, I—"

"But someone else quarrelled with Sir Reuben," continued Poirot in a pensive voice. "Someone else left him that night white with rage. Supposing Lady Astwell left her husband alive at a quarter to twelve that night, there would be ten minutes before Mr. Charles Leverson returned, ten minutes in which it would be possible for someone from the second floor to steal down and do the deed, and then return to his room again."

Victor Astwell sprang up with a cry.

"What the hell—?" He stopped, choking with rage.

"In a rage, Mr. Astwell, you once killed a man in West Africa."

"I don't believe it," cried Lily Margrave.

She came forward, her hands clenched, two bright spots of colour in her cheeks.

"I don't believe it," repeated the girl. She came close to Victor Astwell's side.

"It's true, Lily," said Astwell, "but there are things this man doesn't know. The fellow I killed was a witchdoctor who had just massacred fifteen children. I consider that I was justified."

Lily came up to Poirot.

"M. Poirot," she said earnestly, "you are wrong. Because a man has a sharp temper, because he breaks out and says all kinds of things, that is not any reason why he should do a murder. I know— I *know,* I tell you—that Mr. Astwell is incapable of such a thing."

Poirot looked at her, a very curious smile on his face. Then he took her hand in his and patted it gently.

"You see, Mademoiselle," he said gently, "you also have your intuitions. So you believe in Mr. Astwell, do you?"

Lily spoke quietly.

"Mr. Astwell is a good man," she said, "and he is honest. He had nothing to do with the inside work of the Mpala Gold Fields. He is good through and through, and—I have promised to marry him."

Victor Astwell came to her side and took her other hand.

"Before God, M. Poirot," he said, "I didn't kill my brother."

"I know you did not," said Poirot.

His eyes swept around the room.

"Listen, my friends. In a hypnotic trance, Lady

Astwell mentioned having seen a bulge in the curtain that night."

Everyone's eyes swept to the window.

"You mean there was a burglar concealed there?" exclaimed Victor Astwell. "What a splendid solution!"

"Ah," said Poirot gently. "But it was not *that* curtain."

He wheeled around and pointed to the curtain that masked the little staircase.

"Sir Reuben used the bedroom the night prior to the crime. He breakfasted in bed, and he had Mr. Trefusis up there to give him instructions. I don't know what it was that Mr. Trefusis left in that bedroom, but there was something. When he said good night to Sir Reuben and Lady Astwell, he remembered this thing and ran up the stairs to fetch it. I don't think either the husband or wife noticed him, for they had already begun a violent discussion. They were in the middle of this quarrel when Mr. Trefusis came down the stairs again.

"The things they were saying to each other were of so intimate and personal a nature that Mr. Trefusis was placed in a very awkward position. It was clear to him that they imagined he had left the room some time ago. Fearing to arouse Sir Reuben's anger against himself, he decided to remain where he was and slip out later. He stayed there behind the curtain, and as Lady Astwell left the room she subconsciously noticed the outline of his form there.

"When Lady Astwell had left the room, Trefusis tried to steal out unobserved, but Sir Reuben happened to turn his head, and became aware of the secretary's presence. Already in a bad temper, Sir Reuben hurled abuse at his secretary, and accused him of deliberately eavesdropping and spying.

"Messieurs and Mesdames, I am a student of psychology. All through this case I have looked, not for the bad-tempered man or woman, for bad temper is its own safety valve. He who can bark does not bite. No, I have looked for the good-tempered man, for the man who is patient and self-controlled, for the man who for nine years has played the part of the under dog. There is no strain so great as that which has endured for years, there is no resentment like that which accumulates slowly.

"For nine years Sir Reuben has bullied and browbeaten his secretary, and for nine years that man has endured in silence. But there comes a day when at last the strain reaches its breaking point. *Something snaps!* It was so that night. Sir Reuben sat down at his desk again, but the secretary, instead of turning humbly and meekly to the door, picks up the heavy wooden club, and strikes down the man who had bullied him once too often."

He turned to Trefusis, who was staring at him as though turned to stone.

"It was so simple, your alibi. Mr. Astwell thought you were in your room, but *no one saw you go there.* You were just stealing out after striking down Sir Reuben when you heard a sound, and you hastened back to cover, behind the curtain. You were behind there when Charles Leverson entered the room, you were there when Lily Margrave came. It was not till long after that that you crept up through a silent house to your bedroom. Do you deny it?"

Trefusis began to stammer.

"I—I never—"

"Ah! Let us finish this. For two weeks now I have played the comedy. I have showed you the net closing slowly around you. The fingerprints, footprints, the search of your room with the things artistically replaced. I have struck terror into you with all of this; you have lain awake at night fearing and wondering; did you leave a fingerprint in the room or a footprint somewhere?

"Again and again you have gone over the events of that night wondering what you have done or left undone, and so I brought you to the state where you made a slip. I saw the fear leap into your eyes today when I picked up something from the stairs where you had stood hidden that night. Then I made a great parade, the little box, the entrusting of it to George, and I go out."

Poirot turned towards the door.

"George?"

"I am here, sir."

The valet came forward.

"Will you tell these ladies and gentlemen what my instructions were?"

"I was to remain concealed in the wardrobe in your room, sir, having placed the cardboard box where you told me to. At half past three this afternoon, sir, Mr. Trefusis entered the room; he went to the drawer and took out the box in question."

"And in that box," continued Poirot, "was a common pin. Me, I speak always the truth. I did pick up something on the stairs this morning. That is your English saying, is it not? 'See a pin and pick it up, all the day you'll have good luck.' Me, I have had good luck, I have found the murderer."

He turned to the secretary.

"You see?" he said gently. *"You betrayed yourself."*

Suddenly Trefusis broke down. He sank into a chair sobbing, his face buried in his hands.

"I was mad," he groaned. "I was mad. But, oh, my God, he badgered and bullied me beyond bearing. For years I had hated and loathed him."

"I knew!" cried Lady Astwell.

She sprang forward, her face irradiated with savage triumph.

"I *knew* that man had done it."

She stood there, savage and triumphant.

"And you were right," said Poirot. "One may call things by different names, but the fact remains. Your 'intuition,' Lady Astwell, proved correct. I felicitate you."

Two

The Plymouth Express

I

Alec Simpson, RN, stepped from the platform at Newton Abbot into a first-class compartment of the Plymouth Express. A porter followed him with a heavy suitcase. He was about to swing it up to the rack, but the young sailor stopped him.

"No—leave it on the seat. I'll put it up later. Here you are."

"Thank you, sir." The porter, generously tipped, withdrew.

Doors banged; a stentorian voice shouted: "Plymouth only. Change for Torquay. Plymouth next stop." Then a whistle blew, and the train drew slowly out of the station.

Lieutenant Simpson had the carriage to himself. The December air was chilly, and he pulled up the window. Then he sniffed vaguely, and frowned. What a smell there was! Reminded him of that time in hospital, and the operation on his leg. Yes, chloroform; that was it!

He let the window down again, changing his seat to one with its back to the engine. He pulled a pipe out of his pocket and lit it. For a little time he sat inactive, looking out into the night and smoking.

At last he roused himself, and opening the suitcase, took out some papers and magazines, then closed the suitcase again and endeavoured to shove it under the opposite seat—without success. Some obstacle resisted it. He shoved harder with rising impatience, but it still stuck out halfway into the carriage.

"Why the devil won't it go in?" he muttered, and hauling it out completely, he stooped down and peered under the seat. . . .

A moment later a cry rang out into the night, and the great train came to an unwilling halt in obedience to the imperative jerking of the communication cord.

II

"*Mon ami*," said Poirot, "you have, I know, been deeply interested in this mystery of the Plymouth Express. Read this."

I picked up the note he flicked across the table to me. It was brief and to the point.

Dear Sir,
  I shall be obliged if you will call upon me at your earliest convenience.
  Yours faithfully,
  Ebenezer Halliday

The connection was not clear to my mind, and I looked inquiringly at Poirot.

For answer he took up the newspaper and read aloud: "'A sensational discovery was made last night. A young naval officer returning to Plymouth found under the seat of his compartment the body of a woman, stabbed through the heart. The officer at once pulled the communication cord, and the train was brought to a standstill. The woman, who was about thirty years of age, and richly dressed, has not yet been identified.'

"And later we have this: 'The woman found dead in the Plymouth Express has been identified as the Honourable Mrs. Rupert Carrington.' You see now, my friend? Or if you do not I will add this—Mrs. Rupert Carrington was, before her marriage, Flossie Halliday, daughter of old man Halliday, the steel king of America."

"And he has sent for you? Splendid!"

"I did him a little service in the past—an affair of bearer bonds. And once, when I was in Paris for a royal visit, I had Mademoiselle Flossie pointed out to me. *La jolie petite pensionnaire*! She had the *joli dot* too! It caused trouble. She nearly made a bad affair."

"How was that?"

"A certain Count de la Rochefour. *Un bien mauvais sujet*! A bad hat, as you would say. An adventurer pure and simple, who knew how to appeal to a romantic young girl. Luckily her father got wind of it in time. He took her back to America in haste. I heard of her marriage some years later, but I know nothing of her husband."

"H'm," I said. "The Honourable Rupert Carrington is no beauty, by all accounts. He'd pretty well run through his own money on the turf, and I should imagine old man Halliday's dollars came along in the nick of time. I should say that for a good-looking, well-mannered, utterly unscrupulous young scoundrel, it would be hard to find his mate!"

"Ah, the poor little lady! *Elle n'est pas bien tombée*!"

"I fancy he made it pretty obvious at once that it was her money, and not she, that had attacted him. I believe they drifted apart almost at once. I have heard rumours lately that there was to be a definite legal separation."

"Old man Halliday is no fool. He would tie up her money pretty tight."

"I dare say. Anyway, I know as a fact that the Honourable Rupert is said to be extremely hard up."

"Aha! I wonder—"

"You wonder what?"

"My good friend, do not jump down my throat like that. You are interested, I see. Suppose you accompany me to see Mr. Halliday. There is a taxi stand at the corner."

III

A few minutes sufficed to whirl us to the superb house in Park Lane rented by the American magnate. We were shown into the library, and almost immediately we were joined by a large stout man, with piercing eyes and an aggressive chin.

"M. Poirot?" said Mr. Halliday. "I guess I don't need to tell you what I want you for. You've read the papers, and I'm never one to let the grass grow under my feet. I happened to hear you were in London, and I remembered the good work you did over those bombs. Never forget a name. I've the pick of Scotland Yard, but I'll have my own man as well. Money no object. All the dollars were made for my little girl—and now she's gone, I'll spend my last cent to catch the damned scoundrel that did it! See? So it's up to you to deliver the goods."

Poirot bowed.

"I accept, monsieur, all the more willingly that I saw your daughter in Paris several times. And now I will ask you to tell me the circumstances of her journey to Plymouth and any other details that seem to you to bear upon the case."

"Well, to begin with," responded Halliday, "she wasn't going to Plymouth. She was going to join a house party at Avonmead Court, the Duchess of

Swansea's place. She left London by the twelve-fourteen from Paddington, arriving at Bristol (where she had to change) at two-fifty. The principal Plymouth expresses, of course, run via Westbury, and do not go near Bristol at all. The twelve-fourteen does a non-stop run to Bristol, afterwards stopping at Weston, Taunton, Exeter and Newton Abbot. My daughter travelled alone in her carriage, which was reserved as far as Bristol, her maid being in a third-class carriage in the next coach."

Poirot nodded, and Mr. Halliday went on: "The party at Avonmead Court was to be a very gay one, with several balls, and in consequence my daughter had with her nearly all her jewels—amounting in value, perhaps, to about a hundred thousand dollars."

"*Un moment*," interrupted Poirot. "Who had charge of the jewels? Your daughter, or the maid?"

"My daughter always took charge of them herself, carrying them in a small blue morocco case."

"Continue, monsieur."

"At Bristol the maid, Jane Mason, collected her mistress's dressing bag and wraps, which were with her, and came to the door of Flossie's compartment. To her intense surprise, my daughter told her that she was not getting out at Bristol, but was going on farther. She directed Mason to get out the luggage and put it in the cloakroom. She could have tea in the refreshment room, but she was to wait at the station for her mistress, who would return to Bristol by an up-train in the course of the afternoon. The maid, although very much astonished, did as she was told. She put the luggage in the cloakroom and had some tea. But up-train after up-train came in, and her mistress did not appear. After the arrival of the last train, she left the luggage where it was, and went to a hotel near the station for the night. This morning she read of the tragedy, and returned to town by the first available train."

"Is there nothing to account for your daughter's sudden change of plan?"

"Well there is this: According to Jane Mason, at Bristol, Flossie was no longer alone in her carriage. There was a man in it who stood looking out of the farther window so that she could not see his face."

"The train was a corridor one, of course?"

"Yes."

"Which side was the corridor?"

"On the platform side. My daughter was standing in the corridor as she talked to Mason."

"And there is no doubt in your mind—excuse me!" He got up, and carefully straightened the inkstand which was a little askew. "*Je vous demande pardon*," he continued, re-seating himself. "It affects my nerves to see anything crooked. Strange, is it not? I was saying, monsieur, that there is no doubt in your mind as to this probably unexpected meeting being the cause of your daughter's sudden change of plan?"

"It seems the only reasonable supposition."

"You have no idea as to who the gentleman in question might be?"

The millionaire hesitated for a moment, and then replied: "No—I do not know at all."

"Now—as to the discovery of the body?"

"It was discovered by a young naval officer who at once gave the alarm. There was a doctor on the train. He examined the body. She had been first chloroformed, and then stabbed. He gave it as his opinion that she had been dead about four hours, so it must have been done not long after leaving Bristol—probably between there and Weston, possibly between Weston and Taunton."

"And the jewel case?"

"The jewel case, M. Poirot, was missing."

"One thing more, monsieur. Your daughter's fortune—to whom does it pass at her death?"

"Flossie made a will soon after her marriage, leaving everything to her husband." He hesitated for a minute, and then went on: "I may as well tell you, Monsieur Poirot, that I regard my son-in-law as an unprincipled scoundrel, and that, by my advice, my daughter was on the eve of freeing herself from him by legal means—no difficult matter. I settled her money upon her in such a way that he could not touch it during her lifetime, but although they have lived entirely apart for some years, she had frequently acceded to his demands for money, rather than face an open scandal. However, I was determined to put an end to this. At last Flossie agreed, and my lawyers were instructed to take proceedings."

"And where is Monsieur Carrington?"

"In town. I believe he was away in the country yesterday, but he returned last night."

Poirot considered a little while. Then he said: "I think that is all, monsieur."

"You would like to see the maid, Jane Mason?"

"If you please."

Halliday rang the bell, and gave a short order to the footman.

A few minutes later Jane Mason entered the room, a respectable, hard-featured woman, as emotionless in the face of tragedy as only a good servant can be.

"You will permit me to put a few questions? Your mistress, she was quite as usual before starting yesterday morning? Not excited or flurried?"

"Oh no, sir!"

"But at Bristol she was quite different?"

"Yes, sir, regular upset—so nervous she didn't seem to know what she was saying."

"What did she say exactly?"

"Well, sir, as near as I can remember, she said: 'Mason, I've got to alter my plans. Something has happened—I mean, I'm not getting out here after all. I must go on. Get out the luggage and put it in the cloakroom; then have some tea, and wait for me in the station.'

" 'Wait for you here, ma'am?' I asked.

" 'Yes, yes. Don't leave the station. I shall return by a later train. I don't know when. It mayn't be until quite late.'

" 'Very well, ma'am,' I says. It wasn't my place to ask questions, but I thought it very strange."

"It was unlike your mistress, eh?"

"Very unlike her, sir."

"What do you think?"

"Well, sir, I thought it was to do with the gentleman in the carriage. She didn't speak to him, but she turned round once or twice as though to ask him if she was doing right."

"But you didn't see the gentleman's face?"

"No, sir; he stood with his back to me all the time."

"Can you describe him at all?"

"He had on a light fawn overcoat, and a travelling-cap. He was tall and slender, like and the back of his head was dark."

"You didn't know him?"

"Oh no, I don't think so, sir."

"It was not your master, Mr. Carrington, by any chance?"

Mason looked rather startled.

"Oh, I don't think so, sir!"

"But you are not *sure?*"

"It was about the master's build, sir—but I never thought of it being him. We so seldom saw him . . . I couldn't say it *wasn't* him!"

Poirot picked up a pin from the carpet, and frowned at it severely; then he continued: "Would it be possible for the man to have entered the train at Bristol before you reached the carriage?"

Mason considered.

"Yes, sir, I think it would. My compartment was very crowded, and it was some minutes before I could get out—and then there was a very large crowd on the platform, and that delayed me too. But he'd only have had a minute or two to speak to the mistress, that way. I took it for granted that he'd come along the corridor."

"That is more probable, certainly."

He paused, still frowning.

"You know how the mistress was dressed, sir?"

"The papers give a few details, but I would like you to confirm them."

"She was wearing a white fox fur toque, sir, with a white spotted veil, and a blue frieze coat and skirt—the shade of blue they call electric."

"H'm, rather striking."

"Yes," remarked Mr. Halliday. "Inspector Japp is in hopes that that may help us to fix the spot where the crime took place. Anyone who saw her would remember her."

"*Précisément!*—Thank you, mademoiselle."

113

The maid left the room.

"Well!" Poirot got up briskly. "That is all I can do here—except, monsieur, that I would ask you to tell me everything, but *everything!*"

"I have done so."

"You are sure?"

"Absolutely."

"Then there is nothing more to be said. I must decline the case."

"Why?"

"Because you have not been frank with me."

"I assure you—"

"No, you are keeping something back."

There was a moment's pause, and then Halliday drew a paper from his pocket and handed it to my friend.

"I guess that's what you're after, Monsieur Poirot—though how you know about it fairly gets my goat!"

Poirot smiled, and unfolded the paper. It was a letter written in thin sloping handwriting. Poirot read it aloud.

"*Chère Madame,*
    It is with infinite pleasure that I look forward to the felicity of meeting you again. After your so amiable reply to my letter, I can hardly restrain my impatience. I have never forgotten those days in Paris. It is most cruel that you should be leaving

London tomorrow. However, before very long, and perhaps sooner than you think, I shall have the joy of beholding once more the lady whose image has ever reigned supreme in my heart.

Believe, *chère madame*, all the assurances of my most devoted and unaltered sentiments—

Armand de la Rochefour."

Poirot handed the letter back to Halliday with a bow.

"I fancy, monsieur, that you did not know that your daughter intended renewing her acquaintance with the Count de la Rochefour?"

"It came as a thunderbolt to me! I found this letter in my daughter's handbag. As you probably know, Monsieur Poirot, this so-called count is an adventurer of the worst type."

Poirot nodded.

"But I want to know how you knew of the existence of this letter?"

My friend smiled. "Monsieur, I did not. But to track footmarks and recognize cigarette ash is not sufficient for a detective. He must also be a good psychologist! I knew that you disliked and mistrusted your son-in-law. He benefits by your daughter's death; the maid's description of the mysterious man bears a sufficient resemblance to him. Yet you are not keen on his track! Why?

Surely because your suspicions lie in another direction. Therefore you were keeping something back."

"You're right, Monsieur Poirot. I was sure of Rupert's guilt until I found this letter. It unsettled me horribly."

"Yes. The Count says 'Before very long, and perhaps sooner than you think.' Obviously he would not want to wait until you should get wind of his reappearance. Was it he who travelled down from London by the twelve-fourteen, and came along the corridor to your daughter's compartment? The Count de la Rochefour is also, if I remember rightly, tall and dark!"

The millionaire nodded.

"Well, monsieur, I will wish you good day. Scotland Yard has, I presume, a list of the jewels?"

"Yes, I believe Inspector Japp is here now if you would like to see him."

IV

Japp was an old friend of ours, and greeted Poirot with a sort of affectionate contempt.

"And how are you, monsieur? No bad feeling between us, though we *have* got our different ways of looking at things. How are the 'little grey cells,' eh? Going strong?"

Poirot beamed upon him. "They function, my good Japp; assuredly they do!"

"Then that's all right. Think it was the Honourable Rupert, or a crook? We're keeping an eye on all the regular places, of course. We shall know if the shiners are disposed of, and of course whoever did it isn't going to keep them to admire their sparkle. Not likely! I'm trying to find out where Rupert Carrington was yesterday. Seems a bit of a mystery about it. I've got a man watching him."

"A great precaution, but perhaps a day late," suggested Poirot gently.

"You always will have your joke, Monsieur Poirot. Well, I'm off to Paddington. Bristol, Weston, Taunton, that's my beat. So long."

"You will come round and see me this evening, and tell me the result?"

"Sure thing, if I'm back."

"The good inspector believes in matter in motion," murmured Poirot as our friend departed. "He travels; he measures footprints; he collects mud and cigarette ash! He is extremely busy! He is zealous beyond words! And if I mentioned psychology to him, do you know what he would do, my friend? He would smile! He would say to himself: 'Poor old Poirot! He ages! He grows senile!' Japp is the 'younger generation knocking on the door.' And *ma foi*! They are so busy knocking that they do not notice that the door is open!"

"And what are you going to do?"

"As we have *carte blanche*, I shall expend threepence in ringing up the Ritz—where you may have noticed our Count is staying. After that, as my feet are a little damp, and I have sneezed twice, I shall return to my rooms and make myself a *tisane* over the spirit lamp!"

V

I did not see Poirot again until the following morning. I found him placidly finishing his breakfast.

"Well?" I inquired eagerly. "What has happened?"

"Nothing."

"But Japp?"

"I have not seen him."

"The Count?"

"He left the Ritz the day before yesterday."

"The day of the murder?"

"Yes."

"Then that settles it! Rupert Carrington is cleared."

"Because the Count de la Rochefour has left the Ritz? You go too fast, my friend."

"Anyway, he must be followed, arrested! But what could be his motive?"

"One hundred thousand dollars' worth of jewellery is a very good motive for anyone. No, the question to my mind is: why kill her? Why not simply steal the jewels? She would not prosecute."

118

"Why not?"

"Because she is a woman, *mon ami*. She once loved this man. Therefore she would suffer her loss in silence. And the Count, who is an extremely good psychologist where women are concerned—hence his successes—would know that perfectly well! On the other hand, if Rupert Carrington killed her, why take the jewels which would incriminate him fatally?"

"As a blind."

"Perhaps you are right, my friend. Ah, here is Japp! I recognize his knock."

The inspector was beaming good-humouredly.

"Morning, Poirot. Only just got back. I've done some good work! And you?"

"Me, I have arranged my ideas," replied Poirot placidly.

Japp laughed heartily.

"Old chap's getting on in years," he observed beneath his breath to me. "That won't do for us young folk," he said aloud.

"*Quel dommage?*" Poirot inquired.

"Well, do you want to hear what I've done?"

"You permit me to make a guess? You have found the knife with which the crime was committed, by the side of the line between Weston and Taunton, and you have interviewed the paperboy who spoke to Mrs. Carrington at Weston!"

Japp's jaw fell. "How on earth did you know?

Don't tell me it was those almighty 'little grey cells' of yours!"

"I am glad you admit for once that they are *all mighty!* Tell me, did she give the paperboy a shilling for himself?"

"No, it was half a crown!" Japp had recovered his temper, and grinned. "Pretty extravagant, these rich Americans!"

"And in consequence the boy did not forget her?"

"Not he. Half-crowns don't come his way every day. She hailed him and bought two magazines. One had a picture of a girl in blue on the cover. 'That'll match me,' she said. Oh, he remembered her perfectly. Well, that was enough for me. By the doctor's evidence, the crime *must* have been committed before Taunton. I guessed they'd throw the knife away at once, and I walked down the line looking for it; and sure enough, there it was. I made inquiries at Taunton about our man, but of course it's a big station, and it wasn't likely they'd notice him. He probably got back to London by a later train."

Poirot nodded. "Very likely."

"But I found another bit of news when I got back. They're passing the jewels, all right! That large emerald was pawned last night—by one of the regular lot. Who do you think it was?"

"I don't know—except that he was a short man."

Japp stared. "Well, you're right there. He's short enough. It was Red Narky."

"Who is Red Narky?" I asked.

"A particularly sharp jewel thief, sir. And not one to stick at murder. Usually works with a woman—Gracie Kidd; but she doesn't seem to be in it this time—unless she's got off to Holland with the rest of the swag."

"You've arrested Narky?"

"Sure thing. But mind you, it's the other man we want—the man who went down with Mrs. Carrington in the train. He was the one who planned the job, right enough. But Narky won't squeal on a pal."

I noticed Poirot's eyes had become very green.

"I think," he said gently, "that I can find Narky's pal for you, all right."

"One of your little ideas, eh?" Japp eyed Poirot sharply. "Wonderful how you manage to deliver the goods sometimes, at your age and all. Devil's own luck, of course."

"Perhaps, perhaps," murmured my friend. "Hastings, my hat. And the brush. So! My galoshes, if it still rains! We must not undo the good work of that *tisane. Au revoir*, Japp!"

"Good luck to you, Poirot."

Poirot hailed the first taxi we met, and directed the driver to Park Lane.

When we drew up before Halliday's house, he skipped out nimbly, paid the driver and rang the bell. To the footman who opened the door he made a request in a low voice, and we were immediately taken upstairs. We went up to the top of the house, and were shown into a small neat bedroom.

Poirot's eyes roved round the room and fastened themselves on a small black trunk. He knelt in front of it, scrutinized the labels on it, and took a small twist of wire from his pocket.

"Ask Mr. Halliday if he will be so kind as to mount to me here," he said over his shoulder to the footman.

The man departed, and Poirot gently coaxed the lock of the trunk with a practised hand. In a few minutes the lock gave, and he raised the lid of the trunk. Swiftly he began rummaging among the clothes it contained, flinging them out on the floor.

There was a heavy step on the stairs, and Halliday entered the room.

"What in hell are you doing here?" he demanded, staring.

"I was looking, monsieur, for *this*." Poirot withdrew from the trunk a coat and skirt of bright blue frieze, and a small toque of white fox fur.

"What are you doing with my trunk?" I turned to see that the maid, Jane Mason, had entered the room.

"If you will just shut the door, Hastings. Thank you. Yes, and stand with your back against it.

Now, Mr. Halliday, let me introduce you to Gracie Kidd, otherwise Jane Mason, who will shortly rejoin her accomplice, Red Narky, under the kind escort of Inspector Japp."

VI

Poirot waved a deprecating hand. "It was of the most simple!" He helped himself to more caviar.

"It was the maid's insistence on the clothes that her mistress was wearing that first struck me. Why was she so anxious that our attention should be directed to them? I reflected that we had only the maid's word for the mysterious man in the carriage at Bristol. As far as the doctor's evidence went, Mrs. Carrington might easily have been murdered *before* reaching Bristol. But if so, then the maid must be an accomplice. And if she were an accomplice, she would not wish this point to rest on her evidence alone. The clothes Mrs. Carrington was wearing were of a striking nature. A maid usually has a good deal of choice as to what her mistress shall wear. Now if, after Bristol, anyone saw a lady in a bright blue coat and skirt, and a fur toque, he will be quite ready to swear he had seen Mrs. Carrington.

"I began to reconstruct. The maid would provide herself with duplicate clothes. She and her accomplice chloroform and stab Mrs. Carrington between London and Bristol, probably taking advantage of a tunnel. Her body is rolled under the seat; and the maid takes her place. At Weston she must make herself noticed. How? In all probability, a newspaper boy will be selected. She will insure his remembering her by giving him a large tip. She also drew his attention to the colour of her dress by a remark about one of the magazines. After leaving Weston, she throws the knife out of the window to mark the place where the crime presumably occurred, and changes her clothes, or buttons a long mackintosh over them. At Taunton she leaves the train and returns to Bristol as soon as possible, where her accomplice has duly left the luggage in the cloakroom. He hands over the ticket and himself returns to London. She waits on the platform, carrying out her role, goes to a hotel for the night and returns to town in the morning, exactly as she said.

"When Japp returned from his expedition, he confirmed all my deductions. He also told me that a well-known crook was passing the jewels. I knew that whoever it was would be the exact opposite of the man Jane Mason described. When I heard that it was Red Narky, who always worked with Gracie Kidd—well, I knew just where to find her."

"And the Count?"

"The more I thought of it, the more I was convinced that he had nothing to do with it. That gentleman is much too careful of his own skin to risk murder. It would be out of keeping with his character."

"Well, Monsieur Poirot," said Halliday, "I owe you a big debt. And the cheque I write after lunch won't go near to settling it."

Poirot smiled modestly, and murmured to me: "The good Japp, he shall get the official credit, all right, but though he has got his Gracie Kidd, I think that I, as the Americans say, have got his goat!"

Three

THE AFFAIR AT THE VICTORY BALL

I

Pure chance led my friend Hercule Poirot, formerly chief of the Belgian force, to be connected with the Styles Case. His success brought him notoriety, and he decided to devote himself to the solving of problems in crime. Having been wounded on the Somme and invalided out of the Army, I finally took up my quarters with him in London. Since I have a firsthand knowledge of most of his cases, it has been suggested to me that I select some of the most interesting and place them on record. In doing so, I feel that I cannot do better than begin with that strange tangle which aroused such widespread public interest at the time. I refer to the affair at the Victory Ball.

Although perhaps it is not so fully demonstrative of Poirot's peculiar methods as some of the more obscure cases, its sensational features, the well-known people involved, and the tremendous publicity given it by the press, make it stand out as a *cause célèbre* and I have long felt that it is only fitting that Poirot's connection with the solution should be given to the world.

It was a fine morning in spring, and we were sitting in Poirot's rooms. My little friend, neat and dapper as ever, his egg-shaped head tilted on one side, was delicately applying a new pomade to his moustache. A certain harmless vanity was a characteristic of Poirot's and fell into line with his general love of order and method. The *Daily Newsmonger*, which I had been reading, had slipped to the floor, and I was deep in a brown study when Poirot's voice recalled me.

"Of what are you thinking so deeply, *mon ami*?"

"To tell you the truth," I replied, "I was puzzling over this unaccountable affair at the Victory Ball. The papers are full of it." I tapped the sheet with my finger as I spoke.

"Yes?"

"The more one reads of it, the more shrouded in mystery the whole thing becomes!" I warmed to my subject. "Who killed Lord Cronshaw? Was Coco Courtenay's death on the same night a mere coincidence? Was it an accident? Or did she deliberately take an overdose of cocaine?" I stopped, and then added dramatically: "These are the questions I ask myself."

Poirot, somewhat to my annoyance, did not play up. He was peering into the glass, and merely murmured: "Decidedly, this new pomade, it is a marvel for the moustaches!" Catching my

128

eye, however, he added hastily: "Quite so—and how do you reply to your questions?"

But before I could answer, the door opened, and our landlady announced Inspector Japp.

The Scotland Yard man was an old friend of ours and we greeted him warmly.

"Ah, my good Japp," cried Poirot, "and what brings you to see us?"

"Well, Monsieur Poirot," said Japp, seating himself and nodding to me, "I'm on a case that strikes me as being very much in your line, and I came along to know whether you'd care to have a finger in the pie?"

Poirot had a good opinion of Japp's abilities, though deploring his lamentable lack of method, but I, for my part, considered that the detective's highest talent lay in the gentle art of seeking favours under the guise of conferring them!

"It's the Victory Ball," said Japp persuasively. "Come, now, you'd like to have a hand in that."

Poirot smiled at me.

"My friend Hastings would, at all events. He was just holding forth on the subject, *n'est-ce pas, mon ami*?"

"Well, sir," said Japp condescendingly, "you shall be in it too. I can tell you, it's something of a feather in your cap to have inside knowledge of a case like this. Well, here's to business. You know the main facts of the case, I suppose, Monsieur Poirot?"

"From the papers only—and the imagination of the journalist is sometimes misleading. Recount the whole story to me."

Japp crossed his legs comfortably and began.

"As all the world and his wife knows, on Tuesday last a grand Victory Ball was held. Every twopenny-halfpenny hop calls itself that nowadays, but this was the real thing, held at the Colossus Hall, and all London at it—including your Lord Cronshaw and his party."

"His *dossier*?" interrupted Poirot. "I should say his bioscope—no, how do you call it—biograph?"

"Viscount Cronshaw was fifth viscount, twenty-five years of age, rich, unmarried, and very fond of the theatrical world. There were rumours of his being engaged to Miss Courtenay of the Albany Theatre, who was known to her friends as 'Coco' and who was, by all accounts, a very fascinating young lady."

"Good. *Continuez*!"

"Lord Cronshaw's party consisted of six people: he himself, his uncle, the Honourable Eustace Beltane, a pretty American widow, Mrs. Mallaby, a young actor, Chris Davidson, his wife, and last but not least, Miss Coco Courtenay. It was a fancy dress ball, as you know, and the Cronshaw party represented the old Italian Comedy—whatever that may be."

"The *Commedia dell' Arte*," murmured Poirot. "I know."

"Anyway, the costumes were copied from a set of china figures forming part of Eustace Beltane's collection. Lord Cronshaw was Harlequin; Beltane was Punchinello; Mrs. Mallaby matched him as Pulcinella; the Davidsons were Pierrot and Pierette; and Miss Courtenay, of course, was Columbine. Now, quite early in the evening it was apparent that there was something wrong. Lord Cronshaw was moody and strange in his manner. When the party met together for supper in a small private room engaged by the host, everyone noticed that he and Miss Courtenay were no longer on speaking terms. She had obviously been crying, and seemed on the verge of hysterics. The meal was an uncomfortable one, and as they all left the supper room, she turned to Chris Davidson and requested him audibly to take her home, as she was 'sick of the ball.' The young actor hesitated, glancing at Lord Cronshaw, and finally drew them both back to the supper room.

"But all his efforts to secure a reconciliation were unavailing, and he accordingly got a taxi and escorted the now weeping Miss Courtenay back to her flat. Although obviously very much upset, she did not confide in him, merely reiterating again and again that she would 'make old Cronch sorry for this!' That is the only hint we have that her death might not have been accidental, and it's precious little to go upon. By the time Davidson had quieted her down somewhat, it was too late to return to the Colossus Hall, and Davidson accordingly went straight home to his flat in Chelsea, where his wife arrived shortly afterwards, bearing the news of the terrible tragedy that had occurred after his departure.

"Lord Cronshaw, it seems, became more and more moody as the ball went on. He kept away from his party, and they hardly saw him during the rest of the evening. It was about one-thirty a.m., just before the grand cotillion when everyone was to unmask, that Captain Digby, a brother officer who knew his disguise, noticed him standing in a box gazing down on the scene.

" 'Hullo, Cronch!' he called. 'Come down and be sociable! What are you moping about up there for like a boiled owl? Come along; there's a good old rag coming on now.'

" 'Right!' responded Cronshaw. 'Wait for me, or I'll never find you in the crowd.'

"He turned and left the box as he spoke. Captain Digby, who had Mrs. Davidson with him, waited. The minutes passed, but Lord Cronshaw did not appear. Finally Digby grew impatient.

" 'Does the fellow think we're going to wait all night for him?' he exclaimed.

"At that moment Mrs. Mallaby joined them, and they explained the situation.

" 'Say, now,' cried the pretty widow vivaciously,

'he's like a bear with a sore head tonight. Let's go right away and rout him out.'

"The search commenced, but met with no success until it occurred to Mrs. Mallaby that he might possibly be found in the room where they had supped an hour earlier. They made their way there. What a sight met their eyes! There was Harlequin, sure enough, but stretched on the ground with a table-knife in his heart!"

Japp stopped, and Poirot nodded, and said with the relish of the specialist: *"Une belle affaire*! And there was no clue as to the perpetrator of the deed? But how should there be!"

"Well," continued the inspector, "you know the rest. The tragedy was a double one. Next day there were headlines in all the papers, and a brief statement to the effect that Miss Courtenay, the popular actress, had been discovered dead in her bed, and that her death was due to an overdose of cocaine. Now, was it accident or suicide? Her maid, who was called upon to give evidence, admitted that Miss Courtenay was a confirmed taker of the drug, and a verdict of accidental death was returned. Nevertheless we can't leave the possibility of suicide out of account. Her death is particularly unfortunate, since it leaves us no clue now to the cause of the quarrel the preceding night. By the way, a small enamel box was found on the dead man. It had *Coco* written across it in diamonds, and was half full of cocaine. It was identified by Miss Courtenay's maid as belonging to her mistress, who nearly always carried it about with her, since it contained her supply of the drug to which she was fast becoming a slave."

"Was Lord Cronshaw himself addicted to the drug?"

"Very far from it. He held unusually strong views on the subject of dope."

Poirot nodded thoughtfully.

"But since the box was in his possession, he knew that Miss Courtenay took it. Suggestive, that, is it not, my good Japp?"

"Ah!" said Japp rather vaguely.

I smiled.

"Well," said Japp, "that's the case. What do you think of it?"

"You found no clue of any kind that has not been reported?"

"Yes, there was this." Japp took a small object from his pocket and handed it over to Poirot. It was a small pompon of emerald green silk, with some ragged threads hanging from it, as though it had been wrenched violently away.

"We found it in the dead man's hand, which was tightly clenched over it," explained the inspector.

Poirot handed it back without any comment and asked: "Had Lord Cronshaw any enemies?"

"None that anyone knows of. He seemed a popular young fellow."

"Who benefits by his death?"

"His uncle, the Honourable Eustace Beltane, comes into the title and estates. There are one or two suspicious facts against him. Several people declare that they heard a violent altercation going on in the little supper room, and that Eustace Beltane was one of the disputants. You see, the table-knife being snatched up off the table would fit in with the murder being done in the heat of a quarrel."

"What does Mr. Beltane say about the matter?"

"Declares one of the waiters was the worse for liquor, and that he was giving him a dressing down. Also that it was nearer to one than half past. You see, Captain Digby's evidence fixes the time pretty accurately. Only about ten minutes elapsed between his speaking to Cronshaw and the finding of the body."

"And in any case I suppose Mr. Beltane, as Punchinello, was wearing a hump and a ruffle?"

"I don't know the exact details of the costumes," said Japp, looking curiously at Poirot. "And anyway, I don't quite see what that has got to do with it?"

"No?" There was a hint of mockery in Poirot's smile. He continued quietly, his eyes shining with the green light I had learned to recognize so well: "There was a curtain in this little supper room, was there not?"

"Yes, but—"

"With a space behind it sufficient to conceal a man?"

"Yes—in fact, there's a small recess, but how you knew about it—you haven't been to the place, have you, Monsieur Poirot?"

"No, my good Japp, I supplied the curtain from my brain. Without it, the drama is not reasonable. And always one must be reasonable. But tell me, did they not send for a doctor?"

"At once, of course. But there was nothing to be done. Death must have been instantaneous."

Poirot nodded rather impatiently.

"Yes, yes, I understand. This doctor, now, he gave evidence at the inquest?"

"Yes."

"Did he say nothing of any unusual symptom— was there nothing about the appearance of the body which struck him as being abnormal?"

Japp stared hard at the little man.

"Yes, Monsieur Poirot. I don't know what you're getting at, but he did mention that there was a tension and stiffness about the limbs which he was quite at a loss to account for."

"Aha!" said Poirot. "Aha! *Mon Dieu*! Japp, that gives one to think, does it not?"

I saw that it had certainly not given Japp to think.

"If you're thinking of poison, monsieur, who on earth would poison a man first and then stick a knife into him?"

"In truth that would be ridiculous," agreed Poirot placidly.

"Now is there anything you want to see, monsieur? If you'd like to examine the room where the body was found—"

Poirot waved his hand.

"Not in the least. You have told me the only thing that interests me—Lord Cronshaw's views on the subject of drug taking."

"Then there's nothing you want to see?"

"Just one thing."

"What is that?"

"The set of china figures from which the costumes were copied."

Japp stared.

"Well, you're a funny one!"

"You can manage that for me?"

"Come round to Berkeley Square now if you like. Mr. Beltane—or His Lordship, as I should say now—won't object."

II

We set off at once in a taxi. The new Lord Cronshaw was not at home, but at Japp's request we were shown into the "china room," where the gems of the collection were kept. Japp looked round him rather helplessly.

"I don't see how you'll ever find the ones you want, monsieur."

But Poirot had already drawn a chair in front of the mantelpiece and was hopping up upon it like a nimble robin. Above the mirror, on a small shelf to themselves, stood six china figures. Poirot examined them minutely, making a few comments to us as he did so.

"*Les voilà*! The old Italian Comedy. Three pairs! Harlequin and Columbine, Pierrot and Pierrette—very dainty in white and green—and Punchinello and Pulcinella in mauve and yellow. Very elaborate, the costume of Punchinello—ruffles and frills, a hump, a high hat. Yes, as I thought, very elaborate."

He replaced the figures carefully, and jumped down.

Japp looked unsatisfied, but as Poirot had clearly no intention of explaining anything, the detective put the best face he could upon the matter. As we were preparing to leave, the master of the house came in, and Japp performed the necessary introductions.

The sixth Viscount Cronshaw was a man of about fifty, suave in manner, with a handsome, dissolute face. Evidently an elderly roué, with the languid manner of a poseur. I took an instant dislike to him. He greeted us graciously enough, declaring he had heard great accounts of Poirot's skill, and placing himself at our disposal in every way.

"The police are doing all they can, I know," Poirot said.

"But I much fear the mystery of my nephew's death will never be cleared up. The whole thing seems utterly mysterious."

Poirot was watching him keenly. "Your nephew had no enemies that you know of?"

"None whatever. I am sure of that." He paused, and then went on: "If there are any questions you would like to ask—"

"Only one." Poirot's voice was serious. "The costumes—they were reproduced *exactly* from your figurines?"

"To the smallest detail."

"Thank you, milor'. That is all I wanted to be sure of. I wish you good day."

"And what next?" inquired Japp as we hurried down the street. "I've got to report at the Yard, you know."

"*Bien*! I will not detain you. I have one other little matter to attend to, and then—"

"Yes?"

"The case will be complete."

"What? You don't mean it! You know who killed Lord Cronshaw?"

"*Parfaitement.*"

"Who was it? Eustace Beltane?"

"Ah, *mon ami*, you know my little weakness! Always I have a desire to keep the threads in my own hands up to the last minute. But have no fear. I will reveal all when the time comes. I want no credit—the affair shall be yours, on the condition that you permit me to play out the *dénouement* my own way."

"That's fair enough," said Japp. "That is, if the *dénouement* ever comes! But I say, you *are* an oyster, aren't you?" Poirot smiled. "Well, so long. I'm off to the Yard."

He strode off down the steet, and Poirot hailed a passing taxi.

"Where are we going now?" I asked in lively curiosity.

"To Chelsea to see the Davidsons."

He gave the address to the driver.

"What do you think of the new Lord Cronshaw?" I asked.

"What says my good friend Hastings?"

"I distrust him instinctively."

"You think he is the 'wicked uncle' of the storybooks, eh?"

"Don't you?"

"Me, I think he was most amiable towards us," said Poirot noncommittally.

"Because he had his reasons!"

Poirot looked at me, shook his head sadly, and murmured something that sounded like: "No method."

III

The Davidsons lived on the third floor of a block of "mansion" flats. Mr. Davidson was out, we were told, but Mrs. Davidson was at home. We were ushered into a long, low room with garish Oriental hangings. The air felt close and oppressive, and there was an overpowering fragrance of joss sticks. Mrs. Davidson came to us almost immediately, a small, fair creature whose fragility would have seemed pathetic and appealing had it not been for the rather shrewd and calculating gleam in her light blue eyes.

Poirot explained our connection with the case, and she shook her head sadly.

"Poor Cronch—and poor Coco too! We were both so fond of her, and her death has been a terrible grief to us. What is it you want to ask me? Must I really go over all that dreadful evening again?"

"Oh, madame, believe me, I would not harass your feelings unnecessarily. Indeed, Inspector Japp has told me all that is needful. I only wish to see the costume you wore at the ball that night."

The lady looked somewhat surprised, and Poirot continued smoothly: "You comprehend, madame, that I work on the system of my country. There we always 'reconstruct' the crime. It is possible that I may have an actual *représentation*, and if so, you understand, the costumes would be important."

Mrs. Davidson still looked a bit doubtful.

"I've heard of reconstructing a crime, of course," she said. "But I didn't know you were so particular about details. But I'll fetch the dress now."

She left the room and returned almost immediately with a dainty wisp of white satin and green. Poirot took it from her and examined it, handing it back with a bow.

"*Merci, madame*! I see you have had the misfortune to lose one of your green pompons, the one on the shoulder here."

"Yes, it got torn off at the ball. I picked it up and gave it to poor Lord Cronshaw to keep for me."

"That was after supper?"

"Yes."

"Not long before the tragedy, perhaps?"

A faint look of alarm came into Mrs. Davidson's pale eyes, and she replied quickly: "Oh no—long before that. Quite soon after supper, in fact."

"I see. Well, that is all. I will not derange you further. *Bonjour, madame.*"

"Well," I said as we emerged from the building, "that explains the mystery of the green pompon."

"I wonder."

"Why, what do you mean?"

"You saw me examine the dress, Hastings?"

"Yes?"

"*Eh bien*, the pompon that was missing had not been wrenched off, as the lady said. On the contrary, it had been *cut* off, my friend, cut off with scissors. The threads were all quite even."

"Dear me!" I exclaimed. "This becomes more and more involved."

"On the contrary," replied Poirot placidly, "it becomes more and more simple."

"Poirot," I cried, "one day I shall murder you! Your habit of finding everything perfectly simple is aggravating to the last degree!"

"But when I explain, *mon ami*, is it not always perfectly simple?"

"Yes; that is the annoying part of it! I feel then that I could have done it myself."

"And so you could, Hastings, so you could. If you would but take the trouble of arranging your ideas! Without method—"

"Yes, yes," I said hastily, for I knew Poirot's eloquence when started on his favourite theme only too well. "Tell me, what do we do next? Are you really going to reconstruct the crime?"

"Hardly that. Shall we say that the drama is over, but that I propose to add a—harlequinade?"

IV

The following Tuesday was fixed upon by Poirot as the day for this mysterious performance. The preparations greatly intrigued me. A white screen was erected at one side of the room, flanked by heavy curtains at either side. A man with some lighting apparatus arrived next, and finally a group of members of the theatrical profession, who disappeared into Poirot's bedroom, which had been rigged up as a temporary dressing room.

Shortly before eight, Japp arrived, in no very cheerful mood. I gathered that the official detective hardly approved of Poirot's plan.

"Bit melodramatic, like all his ideas. But there, it can do no harm, and as he says, it might save us a good bit of trouble. He's been very smart over the case. I was on the same scent myself, of course—" I felt instinctively that Japp was straining the truth here—"but there, I promised to let him play the thing out his own way. Ah! Here is the crowd."

His Lordship arrived first, escorting Mrs. Mallaby, whom I had not as yet seen. She was a pretty, dark-haired woman, and appeared perceptibly nervous. The Davidsons followed. Chris Davidson also I saw for the first time. He was handsome enough in a rather obvious style, tall and dark, with the easy grace of the actor.

Poirot had arranged seats for the party facing the screen. This was illuminated by a bright light. Poirot switched out the other lights so that the room was in darkness except for the screen. Poirot's voice rose out of the gloom.

"Messieurs, mesdames, a word of explanation. Six figures in turn will pass across the screen. They are familiar to you. Pierrot and his Pierrette; Punchinello the buffoon, and elegant Pulcinella;

beautiful Columbine, lightly dancing, Harlequin, the sprite, invisible to man!"

With these words of introduction, the show began. In turn each figure that Poirot had mentioned bounded before the screen, stayed there a moment poised, and then vanished. The lights went up, and a sigh of relief went round. Everyone had been nervous, fearing they knew not what. It seemed to me that the proceedings had gone singularly flat. If the criminal was among us, and Poirot expected him to break down at the mere sight of a familiar figure the device had failed signally—as it was almost bound to do. Poirot, however, appeared not a whit discomposed. He stepped forward, beaming.

"Now, messieurs and mesdames, will you be so good as to tell me, one at a time, what it is that we have just seen? Will you begin, milor'?"

The gentleman looked rather puzzled. "I'm afraid I don't quite understand."

"Just tell me what we have been seeing."

"I—er—well, I should say we have seen six figures passing in front of a screen and dressed to represent the personages in the old Italian Comedy, or—er—ourselves the other night."

"Never mind the other night, milor'," broke in Poirot. "The first part of your speech was what I wanted. Madame, you agree with Milor' Cronshaw?"

He had turned as he spoke to Mrs. Mallaby.

"I—er—yes, of course."

"You agree that you have seen six figures representing the Italian Comedy?"

"Why, certainly."

"Monsieur Davidson? You too?"

"Yes."

"Madame?"

"Yes."

"Hastings? Japp? Yes? You are all in accord?"

He looked around upon us; his face grew rather pale, and his eyes were green as any cat's.

"And yet—*you are all wrong!* Your eyes have lied to you—as they lied to you on the night of the Victory Ball. To 'see' things with your eyes, as they say, is not always to see the truth. One must see with the eyes of the mind; one must employ the little cells of grey! Know, then, that tonight and on the night of the Victory Ball, you saw not *six* figures but *five!* See!"

The lights went out again. A figure bounded in front of the screen—Pierrot!

"Who is that?" demanded Poirot. "Is it Pierrot?"

"Yes," we all cried.

"Look again!"

With a swift movement the man divested himself of his loose Pierrot garb. There in the limelight stood glittering Harlequin! At the same moment there was a cry and an overturned chair.

"Curse you," snarled Davidson's voice. "Curse you! How did you guess?"

Then came the clink of handcuffs and Japp's calm official voice. "I arrest you, Christopher Davidson—charge of murdering Viscount Cronshaw—anything you say will be used in evidence against you."

V

It was a quarter of an hour later. A recherché little supper had appeared; and Poirot, beaming all over his face, was dispensing hospitality and answering our eager questions.

"It was all very simple. The circumstances in which the green pompon was found suggested at once that it had been torn from the costume of the murderer. I dismissed Pierrette from my mind (since it takes considerable strength to drive a table-knife home) and fixed upon Pierrot as the criminal. But Pierrot left the ball nearly two hours before the murder was committed. So he must either have returned to the ball later to kill Lord Cronshaw, or—*eh bien*, he must have killed him before he left! Was that impossible? Who had seen Lord Cronshaw after supper that evening? Only Mrs. Davidson, whose statement, I suspected, was a deliberate fabrication uttered with the object of accounting for the missing pompon, which, of course, she cut from her own dress to replace the one missing on her husband's costume. But then, Harlequin, who was seen in the box at one-thirty, must have been an impersonation. For a moment, earlier, I had considered the possibility of Mr. Beltane being the guilty party. But with his elaborate costume, it was clearly impossible that he could have doubled the roles of Punchinello and Harlequin. On the other hand, to Davidson, a young man of about the same height as the murdered man and an actor by profession, the thing was simplicity itself.

"But one thing worried me. Surely a doctor could not fail to perceive the difference between a man who had been dead two hours and one who had been dead ten minutes! *Eh bien*, the doctor *did* perceive it! But he was not taken to the body and asked, 'How long has this man been dead?' On the contrary, he was informed that the man had been seen alive ten minutes ago, and so he merely commented at the inquest on the abnormal stiffening of the limbs for which he was quite unable to account!

"All was now marching famously for my theory. Davidson had killed Lord Cronshaw immediately after supper, when, as you remember, he was seen to draw him back into the supper room. Then he departed with Miss Courtenay, left her at the door of her flat (instead of going in and trying to pacify her as he affirmed) and returned posthaste to the Colossus—but as Harlequin, not Pierrot— a simple transformation effected by removing his outer costume."

VI

The uncle of the dead man leaned forward, his eyes perplexed.

"But if so, he must have come to the ball prepared to kill his victim. What earthly motive could he have had? The motive, that's what I can't get."

"Ah! There we come to the second tragedy— that of Miss Courtenay. There was one simple point which everyone overlooked. Miss Courtenay died of cocaine poisoning—but her supply of the drug was in the enamel box which was found on Lord Cronshaw's body. Where, then, did she obtain the dose which killed her? Only one person could have supplied her with it— Davidson. And that explains everything. It accounts for her friendship with the Davidsons and her demand that Davidson should escort her home. Lord Cronshaw, who was almost fanatically opposed to drug-taking, discovered that she was addicted to cocaine, and suspected that Davidson supplied her with it. Davidson doubtless denied this, but Lord Cronshaw determined to get the truth from Miss Courtenay at the ball. He could forgive the wretched girl, but he would certainly have no mercy on the man who made a living by trafficking in drugs. Exposure and ruin confronted Davidson. He went to the ball determined that Cronshaw's silence must be obtained at any cost."

"Was Coco's death an accident, then?"

"I suspect that it was an accident cleverly engineered by Davidson. She was furiously angry with Cronshaw, first for his reproaches, and secondly for taking her cocaine from her. Davidson supplied her with more, and probably suggested her augmenting the dose as a defiance to 'old Cronch'!"

"One other thing," I said. "The recess and the curtain? How did you know about them?"

"Why, *mon ami*, that was the most simple of all. Waiters had been in and out of that little room, so, obviously, the body could not have been lying where it was found on the floor. There must be some place in the room where it could be hidden. I deduced a curtain and a recess behind it. Davidson dragged the body there, and later, after drawing attention to himself in the box, he dragged it out again before finally leaving the Hall. It was one of his best moves. He is a clever fellow!"

But in Poirot's green eyes I read unmistakably the unspoken remark: "But not quite so clever as Hercule Poirot!"

Four

THE MARKET BASING MYSTERY

I

"After all, there's nothing like the country, is there?" said Inspector Japp, breathing in heavily through his nose and out through his mouth in the most approved fashion.

Poirot and I applauded the sentiment heartily. It had been the Scotland Yard inspector's idea that we should all go for the weekend to the little country town of Market Basing. When off duty, Japp was an ardent botanist, and discoursed upon minute flowers possessed of unbelievably lengthy Latin names (somewhat strangely pronounced) with an enthusiasm even greater than that he gave to his cases.

"Nobody knows us, and we know nobody," explained Japp. "That's the idea."

This was not to prove quite the case, however, for the local constable happened to have been transferred from a village fifteen miles away where a case of arsenical poisoning had brought him into contact with the Scotland Yard man. However, his delighted recognition of the great man only enhanced Japp's sense of well-being, and as we sat down to breakfast on Sunday morning in the parlour of the village inn, with the sun shining, and tendrils of honeysuckle thrusting themselves in at the window, we were all in the best of spirits. The bacon and eggs were excellent, the coffee not so good, but passable and boiling hot.

"This is the life," said Japp. "When I retire, I shall have a little place in the country. Far from crime, like this!"

"*Le crime, il est partout*," remarked Poirot, helping himself to a neat square of bread, and frowning at a sparrow which had balanced itself impertinently on the windowsill.

I quoted lightly:

"That rabbit has a pleasant face,
His private life is a disgrace
I really could not tell to you
The awful things that rabbits do."

"Lord," said Japp, stretching himself backward, "I believe I could manage another egg, and perhaps a rasher or two of bacon. What do you say, Captain?"

"I'm with you," I returned heartily. "What about you, Poirot?"

Poirot shook his head.

"One must not so replenish the stomach that the brain refuses to function," he remarked.

"I'll risk replenishing the stomach a bit more," laughed Japp. "I take a large size in stomachs; and by the way, you're getting stout yourself, M. Poirot. Here, miss, eggs and bacon twice."

At that moment, however, an imposing form blocked the doorway. It was Constable Pollard.

"I hope you'll excuse me troubling the inspector, gentlemen, but I'd be glad of his advice."

"I'm on holiday," said Japp hastily. "No work for me. What is the case?"

"Gentleman up at Leigh House—shot himself—through the head."

"Well, they will do it," said Japp prosaically. "Debt, or a woman, I suppose. Sorry I can't help you, Pollard."

"The point is," said the constable, "that he can't have shot himself. Leastways, that's what Dr. Giles says."

Japp put down his cup.

"*Can't* have shot himself? What do you mean?"

"That's what Dr. Giles says," repeated Pollard. "He says it's plumb impossible. He's puzzled to death, the door being locked on the inside and the windows bolted; but he sticks to it that the man couldn't have committed suicide."

That settled it. The further supply of bacon and eggs was waved aside, and a few minutes later we were all walking as fast as we could in the direction of Leigh House, Japp eagerly questioning the constable.

The name of the deceased was Walter Protheroe; he was a man of middle age and something of a recluse. He had come to Market Basing eight years ago and rented Leigh House, a rambling, dilapidated old mansion fast falling into ruin. He lived in a corner of it, his wants attended to by a housekeeper whom he had brought with him. Miss Clegg was her name, and she was a very superior woman and highly thought of in the village. Just lately Mr. Protheroe had had visitors staying with him, a Mr. and Mrs. Parker from London. This morning, unable to get a reply when she went to call her master, and finding the door locked, Miss Clegg became alarmed, and telephoned for the police and the doctor. Constable Pollard and Dr. Giles had arrived at the same moment. Their united efforts had succeeded in breaking down the oak door of his bedroom.

Mr. Protheroe was lying on the floor, shot through the head, and the pistol was clasped in his right hand. It looked a clear case of suicide.

After examining the body, however, Dr. Giles became clearly perplexed, and finally he drew the constable aside, and communicated his perplexities to him; whereupon Pollard had at once thought of Japp. Leaving the doctor in charge, he had hurried down to the inn.

By the time the constable's recital was over, we had arrived at Leigh House, a big, desolate house surrounded by an unkempt, weed-ridden garden.

The front door was open, and we passed at once into the hall and from there into a small morning room whence proceeded the sound of voices. Four people were in the room: a somewhat flashily dressed man with a shifty, unpleasant face to whom I took an immediate dislike; a woman of much the same type, though handsome in a coarse fashion; another woman dressed in neat black who stood apart from the rest, and whom I took to be the housekeeper; and a tall man dressed in sporting tweeds, with a clever, capable face, and who was clearly in command of the situation.

"Dr. Giles," said the constable, "this is Detective-Inspector Japp of Scotland Yard, and his two friends."

The doctor greeted us and made us known to Mr. and Mrs. Parker. Then we accompanied them upstairs. Pollard, in obedience to a sign from Japp, remained below, as it were on guard over the household. The doctor led us upstairs and along a passage. A door was open at the end; splinters hung from the hinges, and the door itself had crashed to the floor inside the room.

We went in. The body was still lying on the floor. Mr. Protheroe had been a man of middle age, bearded, with hair grey at the temples. Japp went and knelt by the body.

"Why couldn't you leave it as you found it?" he grumbled.

The doctor shrugged his shoulders.

"We thought it a clear case of suicide."

"H'm!" said Japp. "Bullet entered the head behind the left ear."

"Exactly," said the doctor. "Clearly impossible for him to have fired it himself. He'd have had to twist his hand right round his head. It couldn't have been done."

"Yet you found the pistol clasped in his hand? Where is it, by the way?"

The doctor nodded to the table.

"But it wasn't clasped in his hand," he said. "It was inside the hand, but the fingers weren't closed over it."

"Put there afterwards," said Japp; "that's clear enough." He was examining the weapon. "One cartridge fired. We'll test it for fingerprints, but I doubt if we'll find any but yours, Dr. Giles. How long has he been dead?"

"Some time last night. I can't give the time to an hour or so, as those wonderful doctors in detective stories do. Roughly, he's been dead about twelve hours."

So far, Poirot had not made a move of any kind. He had remained by my side, watching Japp at work and listening to his questions. Only, from time to time, he had sniffed the air very delicately, and as if puzzled. I too had sniffed, but could detect nothing to arouse interest. The air seemed perfectly fresh and devoid of odour. And yet, from time to time, Poirot continued to sniff it dubiously, as though his keener nose detected something I had missed.

Now, as Japp moved away from the body, Poirot knelt down by it. He took no interest in the wound. I thought at first that he was examining the fingers of the hand that had held the pistol, but in a minute I saw that it was a handkerchief carried in the coat-sleeve that interested him. Mr. Protheroe was dressed in a dark grey lounge-suit. Finally Poirot got up from his knees, but his eyes still strayed back to the handkerchief as though puzzled.

Japp called to him to come and help to lift the door. Seizing my opportunity, I too knelt down, and taking the handkerchief from the sleeve, scrutinized it minutely. It was a perfectly plain handkerchief of white cambric; there was no mark or stain on it of any kind. I replaced it, shaking my head and confessing myself baffled.

The others had raised the door. I realized that they were hunting for the key. They looked in vain.

"That settles it," said Japp. "The window's shut and bolted. The murderer left by the door, locking it and taking the key with him. He thought it would be accepted that Protheroe had locked himself in and shot himself, and that the absence of the key would not be noticed. You agree, M. Poirot?"

"I agree, yes; but it would have been simpler and better to slip the key back inside the room under the door. Then it would look as though it had fallen from the lock."

"Ah, well, you can't expect everybody to have the bright ideas that you have. You'd have been a holy terror if you'd taken to crime. Any remarks to make, M. Poirot?"

Poirot, it seemed to me, was somewhat at a loss. He looked round the room and remarked mildly and almost apologetically: "He smoked a lot, this monsieur."

True enough, the grate was filled with cigarette stubs, as was an ashtray that stood on a small table near the big armchair.

"He must have got through about twenty cigarettes last night," remarked Japp. Stooping down, he examined the contents of the grate carefully, then transferred his attention to the ashtray. "They're all the same kind," he announced, "and smoked by the same man. There's nothing there, M. Poirot."

"I did not suggest that there was," murmured my friend.

"Ha," cried Japp, "what's this?" He pounced on something bright and glittering that lay on the floor near the dead man. "A broken cuff-link. I wonder who this belongs to. Dr. Giles, I'd be obliged if you'd go down and send up the housekeeper."

"What about the Parkers? He's very anxious to leave the house—says he's got urgent business in London."

"I dare say. It'll have to get on without him. By the way things are going, it's likely that there'll be some urgent business down here for him to attend to! Send up the housekeeper, and don't let either of the Parkers give you and Pollard the slip. Did any of the household come in here this morning?"

The doctor reflected.

"No, they stood outside in the corridor while Pollard and I came in."

"Sure of that?"

"Absolutely certain."

The doctor departed on his mission.

"Good man, that," said Japp approvingly. "Some of these sporting doctors are first-class fellows. Well, I wonder who shot this chap. It looks like one of the three in the house. I hardly suspect the housekeeper. She's had eight years to shoot him in if she wanted to. I wonder who these Parkers are? They're not a prepossessing-looking couple."

Miss Clegg appeared at this juncture. She was a thin, gaunt woman with neat grey hair parted in the middle, very staid and calm in manner. Nevertheless there was an air of efficiency about her which commanded respect. In answer to Japp's questions, she explained that she had been with the dead man for fourteen years. He had been a generous and considerate master. She had never seen Mr. and Mrs. Parker until three days ago, when they arrived unexpectedly to stay. She was of the opinion that they had asked themselves—the master had certainly not seemed pleased to see them. The cuff-links which Japp showed her had not belonged to Mr. Protheroe—she was sure of that. Questioned about the pistol, she said that she believed her master had a weapon of that kind. He kept it locked up. She had seen it once some years ago, but could not say whether this was the same one. She had heard no shot last night, but that was not surprising, as it was a big, rambling house, and her rooms and those prepared for the Parkers were at the other end of the building. She did not know what time Mr. Protheroe had gone to bed—he was still up when she retired at half past nine. It was not his habit to go at once to bed when he went to his room. Usually he would sit up half the night, reading and smoking. He was a great smoker.

Then Poirot interposed a question:

"Did your master sleep with his window open or shut, as a rule?"

Miss Clegg considered.

"It was usually open, at any rate at the top."

"Yet now it is closed. Can you explain that?"

"No, unless he felt a draught and shut it."

Japp asked her a few more questions and then

dismissed her. Next he interviewed the Parkers separately. Mrs. Parker was inclined to be hysterical and tearful; Mr. Parker was full of bluster and abuse. He denied that the cuff-link was his, but as his wife had previously recognized it, this hardly improved matters for him; and as he had also denied ever having been in Protheroe's room, Japp considered that he had sufficient evidence to apply for a warrant.

Leaving Pollard in charge, Japp bustled back to the village and got into telephonic communication with headquarters. Poirot and I strolled back to the inn.

"You're unusually quiet," I said. "Doesn't the case interest you?"

"*Au contraire*, it interests me enormously. But it puzzles me also."

"The motive is obscure," I said thoughtfully, "but I'm certain that Parker's a bad lot. The case against him seems pretty clear but for the lack of motive, and that may come out later."

"Nothing struck you as being especially significant, although overlooked by Japp?"

I looked at him curiously.

"What have you got up your sleeve, Poirot?"

"What did the dead man have up his sleeve?"

"Oh, that handkerchief!"

"Exactly, that handkerchief."

"A sailor carries his handkerchief in his sleeve," I said thoughtfully.

"An excellent point, Hastings, though not the one I had in mind."

"Anything else?"

"Yes, over and over again I go back to the smell of cigarette smoke."

"I didn't smell any," I cried wonderingly.

"No more did I, *cher ami.*"

I looked earnestly at him. It is so difficult to know when Poirot is pulling one's leg, but he seemed thoroughly in earnest and was frowning to himself.

II

The inquest took place two days later. In the meantime other evidence had come to light. A tramp had admitted that he had climbed over the wall into the Leigh House garden, where he often slept in a shed that was left unlocked. He declared that at twelve o'clock he had heard two men quarrelling loudly in a room on the first floor. One was demanding a sum of money; the other was angrily refusing. Concealed behind a bush, he had seen the two men as they passed and repassed the lighted window. One he knew well as being Mr. Protheroe, the owner of the house; the other he identified positively as Mr. Parker.

It was clear now that the Parkers had come to Leigh House to blackmail Protheroe, and when later it was discovered that the dead man's real name was Wendover, and that he had been a lieutenant in the Navy and had been concerned in the blowing up of the first-class cruiser *Merrythought*, in 1910, the case seemed to be rapidly clearing. It was supposed that Parker, cognizant of the part Wendover had played, had tracked him down and demanded hush money which the other refused to pay. In the course of the quarrel, Wendover drew his revolver, and Parker snatched it from him and shot him, subsequently endeavouring to give it the appearance of suicide.

Parker was committed for trial, reserving his defence. We had attended the police-court proceedings. As we left, Poirot nodded his head.

"It must be so," he murmured to himself. "Yes, it must be so. I will delay no longer."

He went into the post office, and wrote off a note which he despatched by special messenger. I did not see to whom it was addressed. Then we returned to the inn where we had stayed on that memorable weekend.

Poirot was restless, going to and from the window.

"I await a visitor," he explained. "It cannot be—surely it cannot be that I am mistaken? No, here she is."

To my utter astonishment, in another minute Miss Clegg walked into the room. She was less calm than usual, and was breathing hard as though she had been running. I saw the fear in her eyes as she looked at Poirot.

"Sit down, mademoiselle," he said kindly. "I guessed rightly, did I not?"

For answer she burst into tears.

"Why did you do it?" asked Poirot gently. "Why?"

"I loved him so," she answered. "I was nurse-maid to him when he was a little boy. Oh, be merciful to me!"

"I will do all I can. But you understand that I cannot permit an innocent man to hang—even though he is an unpleasing scoundrel."

She sat up and said in a low voice: "Perhaps in the end I could not have, either. Do whatever must be done."

Then, rising, she hurried from the room.

"Did she shoot him?" I asked utterly bewildered.

Poirot smiled and shook his head.

"He shot himself. Do you remember that he carried his handkerchief in his *right* sleeve? That showed me that he was left-handed. Fearing exposure, after his stormy interview with Mr. Parker, he shot himself. In the morning Miss Clegg came to call him as usual and found him lying dead. As she has just told us, she had known him from a little boy upward, and was filled with fury against the Parkers, who had driven him to this shameful death. She regarded them as murderers, and then suddenly she saw a chance of making them suffer for the deed they had inspired. She alone knew that he was left-handed. She changed the pistol to his right hand, closed and bolted the window, dropped the bit of cuff-link she had picked up in one of the downstairs rooms, and went out, locking the door and removing the key."

"Poirot," I said, in a burst of enthusiasm, "you are magnificent. All that from the one little clue of the handkerchief."

"And the cigarette smoke. If the window had been closed, and all those cigarettes smoked, the room ought to have been full of stale tobacco. Instead, it was perfectly fresh, so I deduced at once that the window must have been open all night, and only closed in the morning, and that gave me a very interesting line of speculation. I could conceive of no circumstances under which a murderer could want to shut the window. It would be to his advantage to leave it open, and pretend that the murderer had escaped that way, if the theory of suicide did not go down. Of course, the tramp's evidence, when I heard it, confirmed my suspicions. He could never have overheard that conversation unless the window had been open."

"Splendid!" I said heartily. "Now, what about some tea?"

"Spoken like a true Englishman," said Poirot with a sigh. "I suppose it is not likely that I could obtain here a glass of *sirop*?"

Five

THE LEMESURIER INHERITANCE

I

In company with Poirot, I have investigated many strange cases, but none, I think, to compare with that extraordinary series of events which held our interest over a period of many years, and which culminated in the ultimate problem brought to Poirot to solve. Our attention was first drawn to the family history of the Lemesuriers one evening during the war. Poirot and I had but recently come together again, renewing the old days of our acquaintanceship in Belgium. He had been handling some little matter for the War Office— disposing of it to their entire satisfaction; and we had been dining at the Carlton with a Brass Hat who paid Poirot heavy compliments in the intervals of the meal. The Brass Hat had to rush away to keep an appointment with someone, and we finished our coffee in a leisurely fashion before following his example.

As we were leaving the room, I was hailed by a voice which struck a familiar note, and turned to see Captain Vincent Lemesurier, a young fellow whom I had known in France. He was with an older man whose likeness to him proclaimed him to be of the same family. Such proved to be the case, and he was introduced to us as Mr. Hugo Lemesurier, uncle of my young friend.

I did not really know Captain Lemesurier at all intimately, but he was a pleasant young fellow, somewhat dreamy in manner, and I remembered hearing that he belonged to an old and exclusive family with a property in Northumberland which dated from before the Reformation. Poirot and I were not in a hurry, and at the younger man's invitation, we sat down at the table with our two newfound friends, and chattered pleasantly enough on various matters. The elder Lemesurier was a man of about forty, with a touch of the scholar in his stooping shoulders; he was engaged at the moment upon some chemical research work for the Government, it appeared.

Our conversation was interrupted by a tall dark young man who strode up to the table, evidently labouring under some agitation of mind.

"Thank goodness I've found you both!" he exclaimed.

"What's the matter, Roger?"

"Your guv'nor, Vincent. Bad fall. Young horse." The rest trailed off, as he drew the other aside.

In a few minutes our two friends had hurriedly taken leave of us. Vincent Lemesurier's father had had a serious accident while trying a young horse, and was not expected to live until morning.

Vincent had gone deadly white, and appeared almost stunned by the news. In a way, I was surprised—for from the few words he had let fall on the subject while in France, I had gathered that he and his father were not on particularly friendly terms, and so his display of filial feeling now rather astonished me.

The dark young man, who had been introduced to us as a cousin, Mr. Roger Lemesurier, remained behind, and we three strolled out together.

"Rather a curious business, this," observed the young man. "It would interest M. Poirot, perhaps. I've heard of you, you know, M. Poirot—from Higginson." (Higginson was our Brass Hat friend.) "He says you're a whale on psychology."

"I study the psychology, yes," admitted my friend cautiously.

"Did you see my cousin's face? He was absolutely bowled over, wasn't he? Do you know why? A good old-fashioned family curse! Would you care to hear about it?"

"It would be most kind of you to recount it to me."

Roger Lemesurier looked at his watch.

"Lots of time. I'm meeting them at King's Cross. Well, M. Poirot, the Lemesuriers are an old family. Way back in medieval times, a Lemesurier became suspicious of his wife. He found the lady in a compromising situation. She swore that she was innocent, but old Baron Hugo didn't listen.

She had one child, a son—and he swore that the boy was no child of his and should never inherit. I forget what he did—some pleasing medieval fancy like walling up the mother and son alive; anyway, he killed them both, and she died protesting her innocence and solemnly cursing the Lemesuriers forever. No first-born son of a Lemesurier should ever inherit—so the curse ran. Well, time passed, and the lady's innocence was established beyond doubt. I believe that Hugo wore a hair shirt and ended up his days on his knees in a monk's cell. But the curious thing is that from that day to this, no first-born son ever has succeeded to the estate. It's gone to brothers, to nephews, to second sons—never to the eldest son. Vincent's father was the second of five sons, the eldest of whom died in infancy. Of course, all through the war, Vincent has been convinced that whoever else was doomed, he certainly was. But strangely enough, his two younger brothers have been killed, and he himself has remained unscathed."

"An interesting family history," said Poirot thoughtfully. "But now his father is dying, and he, as the eldest son, succeeds?"

"Exactly. A curse has gone rusty—unable to stand the strain of modern life."

Poirot shook his head, as though deprecating the other's jesting tone. Roger Lemesurier looked at his watch again, and declared that he must be off.

The sequel to the story came on the morrow, when we learned of the tragic death of Captain Vincent Lemesurier. He had been travelling north by the Scotch mail-train, and during the night must have opened the door of the compartment and jumped out on the line. The shock of his father's accident coming on top of the shell-shock was deemed to have caused temporary mental aberration. The curious superstition prevalent in the Lemesurier family was mentioned, in connection with the new heir, his father's brother, Ronald Lemesurier, whose only son had died on the Somme.

I suppose our accidental meeting with young Vincent on the last evening of his life quickened our interest in anything that pertained to the Lemesurier family, for we noted with some interest two years later the death of Ronald Lemesurier, who had been a confirmed invalid at the time of his succession to the family estates. His brother John succeeded him, a hale, hearty man with a boy at Eton.

Certainly an evil destiny overshadowed the Lemesuriers. On his very next holiday the boy managed to shoot himself fatally. His father's death, which occurred quite suddenly after being stung by a wasp, gave the estate over to the youngest brother of the five—Hugo, whom we remembered meeting on the fatal night at the Carlton.

Beyond commenting on the extraordinary series of misfortunes which befell the Lemesuriers, we had taken no personal interest in the matter, but the time was now close at hand when we were to take a more active part.

II

One morning "Mrs. Lemesurier" was announced. She was a tall, active woman, possibly about thirty years of age, who conveyed by her demeanour a great deal of determination and strong common sense. She spoke with a faint transatlantic accent.

"M. Poirot? I am pleased to meet you. My husband, Hugo Lemesurier, met you once many years ago, but you will hardly remember the fact."

"I recollect it perfectly, madame. It was at the Carlton."

"That's quite wonderful of you. M. Poirot, I'm very worried."

"What about, Madame?"

"My elder boy—I've two boys, you know. Ronald's eight, and Gerald's six."

"Proceed, madame: why should you be worried about little Ronald?"

"M. Poirot, within the last six months he has had three narrow escapes from death: once from drowning—when we were all down at

Cornwall this summer; once when he fell from the nursery window; and once from ptomaine poisoning."

Perhaps Poirot's face expressed rather too eloquently what he thought, for Mrs. Lemesurier hurried on with hardly a moment's pause: "Of course I know you think I'm just a silly fool of a woman, making mountains out of molehills."

"No, indeed, madame. Any mother might be excused for being upset at such occurrences, but I hardly see where I can be of any assistance to you. I am not *le bon Dieu* to control the waves; for the nursery window I should suggest some iron bars; and for the food—what can equal a mother's care?"

"But why should these things happen to Ronald and not to Gerald?"

"The chance, madame—*le hasard*!"

"You think so?"

"What do you think, madame—you and your husband?"

A shadow crossed Mrs. Lemesurier's face.

"It's no good going to Hugo—he won't listen. As perhaps you may have heard, there's supposed to be a curse on the family—no eldest son can succeed. Hugo believes in it. He's wrapped up in the family history, and he's superstitious to the last degree. When I go to him with my fears, he just says it's the curse, and we can't escape it. But I'm from the States, M. Poirot, and over there we don't believe much in curses. We like them as belonging to a real high-toned old family—it gives a sort of *cachet*, don't you know. I was just a musical comedy actress in a small part when Hugo met me—and I thought his family curse was just too lovely for words. That kind of thing's all right for telling round the fire on a winter's evening, but when it comes to one's own children—I just adore my children, M. Poirot. I'd do anything for them."

"So you decline to believe in the family legend, madame?"

"Can a legend saw through an ivy stem?"

"What is that you are saying, madame?" cried Poirot, an expression of great astonishment on his face.

"I said, can a legend—or a ghost, if you like to call it that—saw through an ivy stem? I'm not saying anything about Cornwall. Any boy might go out too far and get into difficulties—though Ronald could swim when he was four years old. But the ivy's different. Both the boys were very naughty. They'd discovered they could climb up and down by the ivy. They were always doing it. One day—Gerald was away at the time—Ronald did it once too often, and the ivy gave way and he fell. Fortunately he didn't damage himself seriously. But I went out and examined the ivy: it was cut through, M. Poirot—deliberately cut through."

"It is very serious what you are telling me there, madame. You say your younger boy was away from home at the moment?"

"Yes."

"And at the time of the ptomaine poisoning, was he still away?"

"No, they were both there."

"Curious," murmured Poirot. "Now, madame, who are the inmates of your establishment?"

"Miss Saunders, the children's governess, and John Gardiner, my husband's secretary—"

Mrs. Lemesurier paused, as though slightly embarrassed.

"And who else, madame?"

"Major Roger Lemesurier, whom you also met on that night, I believe, stays with us a good deal."

"Ah, yes—he is a cousin is he not?"

"A distant cousin. He does not belong to our branch of the family. Still, I suppose now he is my husband's nearest relative. He is a dear fellow, and we are all very fond of him. The boys are devoted to him."

"It was not he who taught them to climb up the ivy?"

"It might have been. He incites them to mischief often enough."

"Madame, I apologize for what I said to you earlier. The danger is real, and I believe that I can be of assistance. I propose that you should invite us both to stay with you. Your husband will not object?"

"Oh no. But he will believe it to be all of no use. It makes me furious the way he just sits around and expects the boy to die."

"Calm yourself, madame. Let us make our arrangements methodically."

III

Our arrangements were duly made, and the following day saw us flying northward. Poirot was sunk in a reverie. He came out of it, to remark abruptly: "It was from a train such as this that Vincent Lemesurier fell?"

He put a slight accent on the "fell."

"You don't suspect foul play there, surely?" I asked.

"Has it struck you, Hastings, that some of the Lemesurier deaths were, shall we say, capable of being arranged? Take that of Vincent, for instance. Then the Eton boy—an accident with a gun is always ambiguous. Supposing this child had fallen from the nursery window and been dashed to death—what more natural and unsuspicious? But why only the one child, Hastings? Who profits by the death of the elder child? His younger brother, a child of seven! Absurd!"

"They mean to do away with the other later," I

suggested, though with the vaguest ideas as to who "they" were.

Poirot shook his head as though dissatisfied.

"Ptomaine poisoning," he mused. "Atropine will produce much the same symptoms. Yes, there is need for our presence."

Mrs. Lemesurier welcomed us enthusiastically. Then she took us to her husband's study and left us with him. He had changed a good deal since I saw him last. His shoulders stooped more than ever, and his face had a curious pale grey tinge. He listened while Poirot explained our presence in the house.

"How exactly like Sadie's practical common sense!" he said at last. "Remain by all means, M. Poirot, and I thank you for coming; but—what is written, is written. The way of the transgressor is hard. We Lemesuriers *know*—none of us can escape the doom."

Poirot mentioned the sawn-through ivy, but Hugo seemed very little impressed.

"Doubtless some careless gardener—yes, yes, there may be an instrument, but the purpose behind is plain; and I will tell you this, M. Poirot, it cannot be long delayed."

Poirot looked at him attentively.

"Why do you say that?"

"Because I myself am doomed. I went to a doctor last year. I am suffering from an incurable disease—the end cannot be much longer delayed;

but before I die, Ronald will be taken. Gerald will inherit."

"And if anything were to happen to your second son also?"

"Nothing will happen to him; he is not threatened."

"But if it did?" persisted Poirot.

"My cousin Roger is the next heir."

We were interrupted. A tall man with a good figure and crispy curling auburn hair entered with a sheaf of papers.

"Never mind about those now, Gardiner," said Hugo Lemesurier, then he added: "My secretary, Mr. Gardiner."

The secretary bowed, uttered a few pleasant words and then went out. In spite of his good looks, there was something repellent about the man. I said so to Poirot shortly afterward when we were walking round the beautiful old grounds together, and rather to my surprise, he agreed.

"Yes, yes, Hastings, you are right. I do not like him. He is too good-looking. He would be one for the soft job always. Ah, here are the children."

Mrs. Lemesurier was advancing towards us, her two children beside her. They were fine-looking boys, the younger dark like his mother, the elder with auburn curls. They shook hands prettily enough, and were soon absolutely devoted to Poirot. We were next introduced to Miss Saunders, a nondescript female, who completed the party.

IV

For some days we had a pleasant, easy existence—ever vigilant, but without result. The boys led a happy normal life and nothing seemed to be amiss. On the fourth day after our arrival Major Roger Lemesurier came down to stay. He was little changed, still carefree and debonair as of old, with the same habit of treating all things lightly. He was evidently a great favourite with the boys, who greeted his arrival with shrieks of delight and immediately dragged him off to play wild Indians in the garden. I noticed that Poirot followed them unobtrusively.

V

On the following day we were all invited to tea, boys included, with Lady Claygate, whose place adjoined that of the Lemesuriers. Mrs. Lemesurier suggested that we also should come, but seemed rather relieved when Poirot refused and declared he would much prefer to remain at home.

Once everyone had started, Poirot got to work. He reminded me of an intelligent terrier. I believe that there was no corner of the house that he left unsearched; yet it was all done so quietly and methodically that no attention was directed to his movements. Clearly, at the end, he remained unsatisfied. We had tea on the terrace with Miss Saunders, who had not been included in the party.

"The boys will enjoy it," she murmured in her faded way, "though I hope they will behave nicely, and not damage the flower-beds, or go near the bees—"

Poirot paused in the very act of drinking. He looked like a man who has seen a ghost.

"Bees?" he demanded in a voice of thunder.

"Yes, M. Poirot, bees. Three hives. Lady Claygate is very proud of her bees—"

"Bees?" cried Poirot again. Then he sprang from the table and walked up and down the terrace with his hands to his head. I could not imagine why the little man should be so agitated at the mere mention of bees.

At that moment we heard the car returning. Poirot was on the doorstep as the party alighted.

"Ronald's been stung," cried Gerald excitedly.

"It's nothing," said Mrs. Lemesurier. "It hasn't even swollen. We put ammonia on it."

"Let me see, my little man," said Poirot. "Where was it?"

"Here, on the side of my neck," said Ronald importantly. "But it doesn't hurt. Father said: 'Keep still—there's a bee on you.' And I kept still, and he took it off, but it stung me first, though it didn't really hurt, only like a pin, and I didn't cry, because I'm so big and going to school next year."

Poirot examined the child's neck, then drew away again. He took me by the arm and murmured:

"Tonight, *mon ami*, tonight we have a little affair on! Say nothing—to anyone."

He refused to be more communicative, and I went through the evening devoured by curiosity. He retired early and I followed his example. As we went upstairs, he caught me by the arm and delivered his instructions:

"Do not undress. Wait a sufficient time, extinguish your light and join me here."

I obeyed, and found him waiting for me when the time came. He enjoined silence on me with a gesture, and we crept quietly along the nursery wing. Ronald occupied a small room of his own. We entered it and took up our position in the darkest corner. The child's breathing sounded heavy and undisturbed.

"Surely he is sleeping very heavily?" I whispered.

Poirot nodded.

"Drugged," he murmured.

"Why?"

"So that he should not cry out at—"

"At what?" I asked, as Poirot paused.

"At the prick of the hypodermic needle, *mon ami*! Hush, let us speak no more—not that I expect anything to happen for some time."

VI

But in this Poirot was wrong. Hardly ten minutes had elapsed before the door opened softly, and someone entered the room. I heard a sound of quick hurried breathing. Footsteps moved to the bed, and then there was a sudden click. The light of a little electric lantern fell on the sleeping child—the holder of it was still invisible in the shadow. The figure laid down the lantern. With the right hand it brought forth a syringe; with the left it touched the boy's neck—

Poirot and I sprang at the same minute. The lantern rolled to the floor, and we struggled with the intruder in the dark. His strength was extraordinary. At last we overcame him.

"The light, Hastings, I must see his face—though I fear I know only too well whose face it will be."

So did I, I thought as I groped for the lantern. For a moment I had suspected the secretary, egged on by my secret dislike of the man, but I felt assured by now that the man who stood to gain by the death of his two childish cousins was the monster we were tracking.

My foot struck against the lantern. I picked it up and switched on the light. It shone full on the face of—Hugo Lemesurier, the boy's father!

The lantern almost dropped from my hand.

"Impossible," I murmured hoarsely. "Impossible!"

VII

Lemesurier was unconscious. Poirot and I between us carried him to his room and laid him on the bed. Poirot bent and gently extricated something from his right hand. He showed it to me. It was a hypodermic syringe. I shuddered.

"What is in it? Poison?"

"Formic acid, I fancy."

"Formic acid?"

"Yes. Probably obtained by distilling ants. He was a chemist, you remember. Death would have been attributed to the bee sting."

"My God," I muttered. "His own son! And you expected this?"

Poirot nodded gravely.

"Yes. He is insane, of course. I imagine that the family history has become a mania with him. His intense longing to succeed to the estate led him to commit the long series of crimes. Possibly the idea occurred to him first when travelling north that night with Vincent. He couldn't bear the prediction to be falsified. Ronald's son was already dead, and Ronald himself was a dying man—they are a weakly lot. He arranged the accident to the gun, and—which I did not suspect until now—contrived the death of his brother John by this same method of injecting formic acid into the jugular vein. His ambition was realized then, and he became the master of the family acres. But his triumph was short-lived—he found that he was suffering from an incurable disease. And he had the madman's fixed idea—the eldest son of a Lemesurier could not inherit. I suspect that the bathing accident was due to him—he encouraged the child to go out too far. That failing, he sawed through the ivy, and afterwards poisoned the child's food."

"Diabolical!" I murmured with a shiver. "And so cleverly planned!"

"Yes, *mon ami*, there is nothing more amazing than the extraordinary sanity of the insane! Unless it is the extraordinary eccentricity of the sane! I imagine that it is only lately that he has completely gone over the borderline, there was method in his madness to begin with."

"And to think that I suspected Roger—that splendid fellow."

"It was the natural assumption, *mon ami*. We knew that he also travelled north with Vincent that night. We knew, too, that he was the next heir after Hugo and Hugo's children. But our assumption was not borne out by the facts. The ivy was sawn through when only little Ronald was at home—but it would be to Roger's interest that both children should perish. In the same way, it was only Ronald's food that was poisoned. And today when they came home and I found that there was only his father's word for it that Ronald had been stung, I remembered the other death from a wasp sting—and I knew!"

VIII

Hugo Lemesurier died a few months later in the private asylum to which he was removed. His widow was remarried a year later to Mr. John Gardiner, the auburn-haired secretary. Ronald inherited the broad acres of his father, and continues to flourish.

"Well, well," I remarked to Poirot. "Another illusion gone. You have disposed very successfully of the curse of the Lemesuriers."

"I wonder," said Poirot very thoughtfully. "I wonder very much indeed."

"What do you mean?"

"*Mon ami*, I will answer you with one significant word—*red!*"

"Blood?" I queried, dropping my voice to an awe-stricken whisper.

"Always you have the imagination melodramatic, Hastings! I refer to something much more prosaic—the colour of little Ronald Lemesurier's hair."

Six

THE CORNISH MYSTERY

I

"Mrs. Pengelley," announced our landlady, and withdrew discreetly.

Many unlikely people came to consult Poirot, but to my mind, the woman who stood nervously just inside the door, fingering her feather neck-piece, was the most unlikely of all. She was so extraordinarily commonplace—a thin, faded woman of about fifty, dressed in a braided coat and skirt, some gold jewellery at her neck, and with her grey hair surmounted by a singularly unbecoming hat. In a country town you pass a hundred Mrs. Pengelleys in the street every day.

Poirot came forward and greeted her pleasantly, perceiving her obvious embarrassment.

"Madame! Take a chair, I beg of you. My colleague, Captain Hastings."

The lady sat down, murmuring uncertainly: "You are M. Poirot, the detective?"

"At your service, madame."

But our guest was still tongue-tied. She sighed, twisted her fingers, and grew steadily redder and redder.

"There is something I can do for you, eh, madame?"

"Well, I thought—that is—you see—"

"Proceed, madame, I beg of you—proceed."

Mrs. Pengelley, thus encouraged, took a grip on herself.

"It's this way, M. Poirot—I don't want to have anything to do with the police. No, I wouldn't go to the police for anything! But all the same, I'm sorely troubled about something. And yet I don't know if I ought—" She stopped abruptly.

"Me, I have nothing to do with the police. My investigations are strictly private."

Mrs. Pengelley caught at the word.

"Private—that's what I want. I don't want any talk or fuss, or things in the papers. Wicked it is, the way they write things, until the family could never hold up their heads again. And it isn't as though I was even sure—it's just a dreadful idea that's come to me, and put it out of my head I can't." She paused for breath. "And all the time I may be wickedly wronging poor Edward. It's a terrible thought for any wife to have. But you do read of such dreadful things nowadays."

"Permit me—it is of your husband you speak?"

"Yes."

"And you suspect him of—what?"

"I don't like even to say it, M. Poirot. But you *do* read of such things happening—and the poor souls suspecting nothing."

I was beginning to despair of the lady's ever coming to the point, but Poirot's patience was equal to the demand made upon it.

"Speak without fear, madame. Think what joy will be yours if we are able to prove your suspicions unfounded."

"That's true—anything's better than this wearing uncertainty. Oh, M. Poirot, I'm dreadfully afraid I'm being *poisoned*."

"What makes you think so?"

Mrs. Pengelley, her reticence leaving her, plunged into a full recital more suited to the ears of her medical attendant.

"Pain and sickness after food, eh?" said Poirot thoughtfully. "You have a doctor attending you, madame? What does he say?"

"He says it's acute gastritis, M. Poirot. But I can see that he's puzzled and uneasy, and he's always altering the medicine, but nothing does any good."

"You have spoken of your—fears, to him?"

"No, indeed, M. Poirot. It might get about in the town. And perhaps it *is gastritis*. All the same, it's very odd that whenever Edward is away for the weekend, I'm quite all right again. Even Freda notices that—my niece, M. Poirot. And then there's that bottle of weed killer, never used, the gardener says, and yet it's half-empty."

She looked appealingly at Poirot. He smiled reassuringly at her, and reached for a pencil and notebook.

"Let us be businesslike, madame. Now, then, you and your husband reside—where?"

"Polgarwith, a small market town in Cornwall."

"You have lived there long?"

"Fourteen years."

"And your household consists of you and your husband. Any children?"

"No."

"But a niece, I think you said?"

"Yes, Freda Stanton, the child of my husband's only sister. She has lived with us for the last eight years—that is, until a week ago."

"Oh, and what happened a week ago?"

"Things hadn't been very pleasant for some time; I don't know what had come over Freda. She was so rude and impertinent, and her temper something shocking, and in the end she flared up one day, and out she walked and took rooms of her own in the town. I've not seen her since. Better leave her to come to her senses, so Mr. Radnor says."

"Who is Mr. Radnor?"

Some of Mrs. Pengelley's initial embarrassment returned.

"Oh, he's—he's just a friend. Very pleasant young fellow."

"Anything between him and your niece?"

"Nothing whatever," said Mrs. Pengelley emphatically.

Poirot shifted his ground.

"You and your husband are, I presume, in comfortable circumstances?"

"Yes, we're very nicely off."

"The money, is it yours or your husband's?"

"Oh, it's all Edward's. I've nothing of my own."

"You see, madame, to be businesslike, we must be brutal. We must seek for a motive. Your husband, he would not poison you just *pour passer le temps*! Do you know of any reason why he should wish you out of the way?"

"There's the yellow-haired hussy who works for him," said Mrs. Pengelley, with a flash of temper. "My husband's a dentist, M. Poirot, and nothing would do but he must have a smart girl, as he said, with bobbed hair and a white overall, to make his appointments and mix his fillings for him. It's come to my ears that there have been fine goings-on, though of course he swears it's all right."

"This bottle of weed killer, madame, who ordered it?"

"My husband—about a year ago."

"Your niece, now, has she any money of her own?"

"About fifty pounds a year, I should say. She'd be glad enough to come back and keep house for Edward if I left him."

"You have contemplated leaving him, then?"

"I don't intend to let him have it all his own

way. Women aren't the downtrodden slaves they were in the old days, M. Poirot."

"I congratulate you on your independent spirit, madame; but let us be practical. You return to Polgarwith today?"

"Yes, I came up by an excursion. Six this morning the train started, and the train goes back at five this afternoon."

"*Bien*! I have nothing of great moment on hand. I can devote myself to your little affair. Tomorrow I shall be in Polgarwith. Shall we say that Hastings, here, is a distant relative of yours, the son of your second cousin? Me, I am his eccentric foreign friend. In the meantime, eat only what is prepared by your own hands, or under your eye. You have a maid whom you trust?"

"Jessie is a very good girl, I am sure."

"Till tomorrow then, madame, and be of good courage."

II

Poirot bowed the lady out, and returned thoughtfully to his chair. His absorption was not so great, however, that he failed to see two minute strands of feather scarf wrenched off by the lady's agitated fingers. He collected them carefully and consigned them to the wastepaper basket.

"What do you make of the case, Hastings?"

"A nasty business, I should say."

"Yes, if what the lady suspects be true. But is it? Woe betide any husband who orders a bottle of weed killer nowadays. If his wife suffers from gastritis, and is inclined to be of a hysterical temperament, the fat is in the fire."

"You think that is all there is to it?"

"Ah—*voilà*—I do not know, Hastings. But the case interests me—it interests me enormously. For, you see, it has positively no new features. Hence the hysterical theory, and yet Mrs. Pengelley did not strike me as being a hysterical woman. Yes, if I mistake not, we have here a very poignant human drama. Tell me, Hastings, what do you consider Mrs. Pengelley's feelings towards her husband to be?"

"Loyalty struggling with fear," I suggested.

"Yet, ordinarily, a woman will accuse anyone in the world—but not her husband. She will stick to her belief in him through thick and thin."

"The 'other woman' complicates the matter."

"Yes, affection may turn to hate, under the stimulus of jealousy. But hate would take her to the police—not to me. She would want an outcry—a scandal. No, no, let us exercise our little grey cells. Why did she come to me? To have her suspicions proved wrong? Or—to have them *proved right?* Ah, we have here something I do not understand—an unknown factor. Is she a superb actress, our Mrs. Pengelley? No, she was genuine, I would swear that she was genuine, and therefore I am interested. Look up the trains to Polgarwith, I pray you."

III

The best train of the day was the one-fifty from Paddington which reached Polgarwith just after seven o'clock. The journey was uneventful, and I had to rouse myself from a pleasant nap to alight upon the platform of the bleak little station. We took our bags to the Duchy Hotel, and after a light meal, Poirot suggested our stepping round to pay an after-dinner call on my so-called cousin.

The Pengelleys' house stood a little way back from the road with an old-fashioned cottage garden in front. The smell of stocks and mignonette came sweetly wafted on the evening breeze. It seemed impossible to associate thoughts of violence with this Old World charm. Poirot rang and knocked. As the summons was not answered, he rang again. This time, after a little pause, the door was opened by a dishevelled-looking servant. Her eyes were red, and she was sniffing violently.

"We wish to see Mrs. Pengelley," explained Poirot. "May we enter?"

The maid stared. Then, with unusual directness, she answered: "Haven't you heard, then? She's dead. Died this evening—about half an hour ago."

We stood staring at her, stunned.

"What did she die of?" I asked at last.

"There's some as could tell." She gave a quick glance over her shoulder. "If it wasn't that somebody ought to be in the house with the missus, I'd pack my box and go tonight. But I'll not leave her dead with no one to watch by her. It's not my place to say anything, and I'm not going to say anything—but everybody knows. It's all over the town. And if Mr. Radnor don't write to the 'Ome Secretary, someone else will. The doctor may say what he likes. Didn't I see the master with my own eyes a-lifting down of the weed killer from the shelf this very evening? And didn't he jump when he turned round and saw me watching of him? And the missus' gruel there on the table, all ready to take to her? Not another bit of food passes my lips while I am in this house! Not if I dies for it."

"Where does the doctor live who attended your mistress?"

"Dr. Adams. Round the corner in High Street. The second house."

Poirot turned away abruptly. He was very pale.

"For a girl who was not going to say anything, that girl said a lot," I remarked dryly.

Poirot struck his clenched hand into his palm.

"An imbecile, a criminal imbecile, that is what I have been, Hastings. I have boasted of my little grey cells, and now I have lost a human life, a life that came to me to be saved. Never did I dream that anything would happen so soon. May the good God forgive me, but I never believed anything would happen at all. Her story seemed to me artificial. Here we are at the doctor's. Let us see what he can tell us."

IV

Dr. Adams was the typical genial red-faced country doctor of fiction. He received us politely enough, but at a hint of our errand, his red face became purple.

"Damned nonsense! Damned nonsense, every word of it! Wasn't I in attendance on the case? Gastritis—gastritis pure and simple. This town's a hotbed of gossip—a lot of scandal-mongering old women get together and invent God knows what. They read these scurrilous rags of newspapers, and nothing will suit them but that someone in their town shall get poisoned too. They see a bottle of weed killer on a shelf—and hey presto!—away goes their imagination with the bit between his teeth. I know Edward Pengelley—he wouldn't poison his grandmother's dog. And why should he poison his wife? Tell me that?"

"There is one thing, *M. le Docteur*, that perhaps you do not know."

And, very briefly, Poirot outlined the main facts of Mrs. Pengelley's visit to him. No one could have been more astonished than Dr. Adams. His eyes almost started out of his head.

"God bless my soul!" he ejaculated. "The poor woman must have been mad. Why didn't she speak to me? That was the proper thing to do."

"And have her fears ridiculed?"

"Not at all, not at all. I hope I've got an open mind."

Poirot looked at him and smiled. The physician was evidently more perturbed than he cared to admit. As we left the house, Poirot broke into a laugh.

"He is as obstinate as a pig, that one. He has said it is gastritis; therefore it is gastritis! All the same, he has the mind uneasy."

"What's our next step?"

"A return to the inn, and a night of horror upon one of your English provincial beds, *mon ami*. It is a thing to make pity, the cheap English bed!"

"And tomorrow?"

"*Rien à faire.* We must return to town and await developments."

"That's very tame," I said, disappointed. "Suppose there are none?"

"There will be! I promise you that. Our old doctor may give as many certificates as he pleases. He cannot stop several hundred tongues from wagging. And they will wag to some purpose, I can tell you that!"

Our train for town left at eleven the following

morning. Before we started for the station, Poirot expressed a wish to see Miss Freda Stanton, the niece mentioned to us by the dead woman. We found the house where she was lodging easily enough. With her was a tall, dark young man whom she introduced in some confusion as Mr. Jacob Radnor.

Miss Freda Stanton was an extremely pretty girl of the old Cornish type—dark hair and eyes and rosy cheeks. There was a flash in those same dark eyes which told of a temper that it would not be wise to provoke.

"Poor Auntie," she said, when Poirot had introduced himself, and explained his business. "It's terribly sad. I've been wishing all the morning that I'd been kinder and more patient."

"You stood a great deal, Freda," interrupted Radnor.

"Yes, Jacob, but I've got a sharp temper, I know. After all, it was only silliness on Auntie's part. I ought to have just laughed and not minded. Of course, it's all nonsense her thinking that Uncle was poisoning her. She *was* worse after any food he gave her—but I'm sure it was only from thinking about it. She made up her mind she would be, and then she was."

"What was the actual cause of your disagreement, mademoiselle?"

Miss Stanton hesitated, looking at Radnor. That young gentleman was quick to take the hint.

"I must be getting along, Freda. See you this evening. Good-bye, gentlemen; you're on your way to the station, I suppose?"

Poirot replied that we were, and Radnor departed.

"You are affianced, is it not so?" demanded Poirot, with a sly smile.

Freda Stanton blushed and admitted that such was the case.

"And that was really the whole trouble with Auntie," she added.

"She did not approve of the match for you?"

"Oh, it wasn't that so much. But you see, she—" The girl came to a stop.

"Yes?" encouraged Poirot gently.

"It seems rather a horrid thing to say about her—now she's dead. But you'll never understand unless I tell you. Auntie was absolutely infatuated with Jacob."

"Indeed?"

"Yes, wasn't it absurd? She was over fifty, and he's not quite thirty! But there it was. She was silly about him! I had to tell her at last that it was me he was after—and she carried on dreadfully. She wouldn't believe a word of it, and was so rude and insulting that it's no wonder I lost my temper. I talked it over with Jacob, and we agreed that the best thing to do was for me to clear out for a bit till she came to her senses. Poor Auntie—I suppose she was in a queer state altogether."

"It would certainly seem so. Thank you, mademoiselle, for making things so clear to me."

V

A little to my surprise, Radnor was waiting for us in the street below.

"I can guess pretty well what Freda has been telling you," he remarked. "It was a most unfortunate thing to happen, and very awkward for me, as you can imagine. I need hardly say that it was none of my doing. I was pleased at first, because I imagined the old woman was helping on things with Freda. The whole thing was absurd—but extremely unpleasant."

"When are you and Miss Stanton going to be married?"

"Soon, I hope. Now, M. Poirot, I'm going to be candid with you. I know a bit more than Freda does. She believes her uncle to be innocent. I'm not so sure. But I can tell you one thing: I'm going to keep my mouth shut about what I do know. Let sleeping dogs lie. I don't want my wife's uncle tried and hanged for murder."

"Why do you tell me all this?"

"Because I've heard of you, and I know you're a clever man. It's quite possible that you might ferret out a case against him. But I put it to you—what good is that? The poor woman is past help, and she'd have been the last person to want a scandal—why, she'd turn in her grave at the mere thought of it."

"You are probably right there. You want me to—hush it up, then?"

"That's my idea. I'll admit frankly that I'm selfish about it. I've got my way to make—and I'm building up a good little business as a tailor and outfitter."

"Most of us are selfish, Mr. Radnor. Not all of us admit it so freely. I will do what you ask—but I tell you frankly you will not succeed in hushing it up."

"Why not?"

Poirot held up a finger. It was market day, and we were passing the market—a busy hum came from within.

"The voice of the people—that is why, Mr. Radnor. Ah, we must run, or we shall miss our train."

VI

"Very interesting, is it not, Hastings?" said Poirot, as the train steamed out of the station.

He had taken out a small comb from his pocket, also a microscopic mirror, and was carefully arranging his moustache, the symmetry of which had become slightly impaired during our brisk run.

"You seem to find it so," I replied. "To me, it is all rather sordid and unpleasant. There's hardly any mystery about it."

"I agree with you; there is no mystery whatever."

"I suppose we can accept the girl's rather extraordinary story of her aunt's infatuation? That seemed the only fishy part to me. She was such a nice, respectable woman."

"There is nothing extraordinary about that—it is completely ordinary. If you read the papers carefully, you will find that often a nice respectable woman of that age leaves a husband she has lived with for twenty years, and sometimes a whole family of children as well, in order to link her life with that of a young man considerably her junior. You admire *les femmes*, Hastings; you prostrate yourself before all of them who are good-looking and have the good taste to smile upon you; but psychologically you know nothing whatever about them. In the autumn of a woman's life, there comes always one mad moment when she longs for romance, for adventure—before it is too late. It comes none the less surely to a woman because she is the wife of a respectable dentist in a country town!"

"And you think—"

"That a clever man might take advantage of such a moment."

"I shouldn't call Pengelley so clever," I mused.

"He's got the whole town by the ears. And yet I suppose you're right. The only two men who know anything, Radnor and the doctor, both want to hush it up. He's managed that somehow. I wish we'd seen the fellow."

"You can indulge your wish. Return by the next train and invent an aching molar."

I looked at him keenly.

"I wish I knew what you considered so interesting about the case."

"My interest is very aptly summed up by a remark of yours, Hastings. After interviewing the maid, you observed that for someone who was not going to say a word, she had said a good deal."

"Oh!" I said doubtfully; then I harped back to my original criticism: "I wonder why you made no attempt to see Pengelley?"

"*Mom ami*, I give him just three months. Then I shall see him for as long as I please—in the dock."

VII

For once I thought Poirot's prognostications were going to be proved wrong. The time went by, and nothing transpired as to our Cornish case. Other matters occupied us, and I had nearly forgotten the Pengelley tragedy when it was suddenly recalled to me by a short paragraph in the paper which stated that an order to exhume the body of Mrs. Pengelley had been obtained from the Home Secretary.

A few days later, and "The Cornish Mystery" was the topic of every paper. It seemed that gossip had never entirely died down, and when the engagement of the widower to Miss Marks, his secretary, was announced, the tongues burst out again louder than ever. Finally a petition was sent to the Home Secretary; the body was exhumed; large quantities of arsenic were discovered; and Mr. Pengelley was arrested and charged with the murder of his wife.

Poirot and I attended the preliminary proceedings. The evidence was much as might have been expected. Dr. Adams admitted that the symptoms of arsenical poisoning might easily be mistaken for those of gastritis. The Home Office expert gave his evidence; the maid Jessie poured out a flood of voluble information, most of which was rejected, but which certainly strengthened the case against the prisoner. Freda Stanton gave evidence as to her aunt's being worse whenever she ate food prepared by her husband. Jacob Radnor told how he had dropped in unexpectedly on the day of Mrs. Pengelley's death, and found Pengelley replacing the bottle of weed killer on the pantry shelf, Mrs. Pengelley's gruel being on the table close by. Then Miss Marks, the fair-haired secretary, was called, and wept and went into hysterics and admitted that there had been "passages" between her and her employer, and that he had promised to marry her in the event of anything happening to his wife. Pengelley reserved his defence and was sent for trial.

VIII

Jacob Radnor walked back with us to our lodgings.

"You see, Mr. Radnor," said Poirot, "I was right. The voice of the people spoke—and with no uncertain voice. There was to be no hushing up of this case."

"You were quite right," sighed Radnor. "Do you see any chance of his getting off?"

"Well, he has reserved his defence. He may have something—up the sleeves, as you English say. Come in with us, will you not?"

Radnor accepted the invitation. I ordered two whiskies and sodas and a cup of chocolate. The last order caused consternation, and I much doubted whether it would ever put in an appearance.

"Of course," continued Poirot, "I have a good deal of experience in matters of this kind. And I see only one loophole of escape for our friend."

"What is it?"

"That you should sign this paper."

With the suddenness of a conjuror, he produced a sheet of paper covered with writing.

"What is it?"

"A confession that *you* murdered Mrs. Pengelley."

There was a moment's pause; then Radnor laughed.

"You must be mad!"

"No, no, my friend, I am not mad. You came here; you started a little business; you were short of money. Mr. Pengelley was a man very well-to-do. You met his niece; she was inclined to smile upon you. But the small allowance that Pengelley might have given her upon her marriage was not enough for you. You must get rid of both the uncle and the aunt; then the money would come to her, since she was the only relative. How cleverly you set about it! You made love to that plain middle-aged woman until she was your slave. You implanted in her doubts of her husband. She discovered first that he was deceiving her—then, under your guidance, that he was trying to poison her. You were often at the house; you had opportunities to introduce the arsenic into her food. But you were careful never to do so when her husband was away. Being a woman, she did not keep her suspicions to herself. She talked to her niece; doubtless she talked to other women friends. Your only difficulty was keeping up separate relations with the two women, and even that was not so difficult as it looked. You explained to the aunt that, to allay the suspicions of her husband, you had to pretend to pay court to the niece. And the younger lady needed little convincing—she would never seriously consider her aunt as a rival.

"But then Mrs. Pengelley made up her mind, without saying anything to you, to consult *me*. If she could be really assured, beyond any possible doubt, that her husband was trying to poison her, she would feel justified in leaving him, and linking her life with yours—which is what she imagined you wanted her to do. But that did not suit your book at all. You did not want a detective prying around. A favourable minute occurs. You are in the house when Mr. Pengelley is getting some gruel for his wife, and you introduce the fatal dose. The rest is easy. Apparently anxious to hush matters up, you secretly foment them. But you reckoned without Hercule Poirot, my intelligent young friend."

Radnor was deadly pale, but he still endeavoured to carry off matters with a high hand.

"Very interesting and ingenious, but why tell me all this?"

"Because, monsieur, I represent—not the law, but Mrs. Pengelley. For her sake, I give you a chance of escape. Sign this paper, and you shall have twenty-four hours' start—twenty-four hours before I place it in the hands of the police."

Radnor hesitated.

"You can't prove anything."

"Can't I? I am Hercule Poirot. Look out of the window, monsieur. There are two men in the street. They have orders not to lose sight of you."

Radnor strode across to the window and pulled aside the blind, then shrank back with an oath.

"You see, monsieur? Sign—it is your best chance."

"What guarantee have I—"

"That I shall keep faith? The word of Hercule Poirot. You will sign? Good. Hastings, be so kind as to pull that left-hand blind halfway up. That is the signal that Mr. Radnor may leave unmolested."

White, muttering oaths, Radnor hurried from the room. Poirot nodded gently.

"A coward! I always knew it."

"It seems to me, Poirot, that you've acted in a criminal manner," I cried angrily. "You always preach against sentiment. And here you are letting a dangerous criminal escape out of sheer sentimentality."

"That was not sentiment—that was business," replied Poirot. "Do you not see, my friend, that we have no shadow of proof against him? Shall I get up and say to twelve stolid Cornishmen that *I*, Hercule Poirot, *know?* They would laugh at me. The only chance was to frighten him and get a confession that way. Those two loafers that I noticed outside came in very useful. Pull down the blind again, will you, Hastings. Not that there was any reason for raising it. It was part of our *mise en scène.*

"Well, well, we must keep our word. Twenty-four hours, did I say? So much longer for poor Mr. Pengelley—and it is not more than he deserves; for mark you, he deceived his wife. I am very strong on the family life, as you know. Ah, well, twenty-four hours—and then? I have great faith in Scotland Yard. They will get him, *mon ami*; they will get him."

Seven

THE KING OF CLUBS

I

"Truth," I observed, laying aside the *Daily Newsmonger*, "is stranger than fiction!"

The remark was not, perhaps, an original one. It appeared to incense my friend. Tilting his egg-shaped head on one side, the little man carefully flicked an imaginary fleck of dust from his carefully creased trousers, and observed: "How profound! What a thinker is my friend Hastings!"

Without displaying any annoyance at this quite uncalled-for gibe, I tapped the sheet I had laid aside.

"You've read this morning's paper?"

"I have. And after reading it, I folded it anew symmetrically. I did not cast it on the floor as you have done, with your so lamentable absence of order and method."

(That is the worst of Poirot. Order and Method are his gods. He goes so far as to attribute all his success to them.)

"Then you saw the account of the murder of Henry Reedburn, the impresario? It was that which prompted my remark. Not only is truth stranger than fiction—it is more dramatic. Think of that solid middle-class English family, the Oglanders. Father and mother, son and daughter, typical of thousands of families all over this country. The men of the family go to the city every day; the women look after the house. Their lives are perfectly peaceful, and utterly monotonous. Last night they were sitting in their neat suburban drawing room at Daisymead, Streatham, playing bridge. Suddenly, without any warning, the french window bursts open, and a woman staggers into the room. Her grey satin frock is marked with a crimson stain. She utters one word, "Murder!" before she sinks to the ground insensible. It is possible that they recognize her from her pictures as Valerie Saintclair, the famous dancer who has lately taken London by storm!"

"Is this your eloquence, or that of the *Daily Newsmonger*?" inquired Poirot.

"The *Daily Newsmonger* was in a hurry to go to press, and contented itself with bare facts. But the dramatic possibilities of the story struck me at once."

Poirot nodded thoughtfully. "Wherever there is human nature, there is drama. *But*—it is not always just where you think it is. Remember that. Still, I too am interested in the case, since it is likely that I shall be connected with it."

"Indeed?"

"Yes. A gentleman rang me up this morning, and made an appointment with me on behalf of Prince Paul of Maurania."

"But what has that to do with it?"

"You do not read your pretty little English scandal-papers. The ones with the funny stories, and 'a little mouse has heard—' or 'a little bird would like to know—' See here."

I followed his short stubby finger along the paragraph: "—whether the foreign prince and the famous dancer are *really* affinities! And if the lady likes her new diamond ring!"

"And now to resume your so dramatic narrative," said Poirot. "Mademoiselle Saintclair had just fainted on the drawing room carpet at Daisymead, you remember."

I shrugged. "As a result of Mademoiselle's first murmured words when she came round, the two male Oglanders stepped out, one to fetch a doctor to attend to the lady, who was evidently suffering terribly from shock, and the other to the police station—whence after telling his story, he accompanied the police to Mon Désir, Mr. Reedburn's magnificent villa, which is situated at no great distance from Daisymead. There they found the great man, who by the way suffers from a somewhat unsavoury reputation, lying in the library with the back of his head cracked open like an eggshell."

"I have cramped your style," said Poirot

kindly. "Forgive me, I pray . . . Ah, here is *M. le Prince*!"

Our distinguished visitor was announced under the title of Count Feodor. He was a strange-looking youth, tall, eager, with a weak chin, the famous Mauranberg mouth, and the dark fiery eyes of a fanatic.

"M. Poirot?"

My friend bowed.

"Monsieur, I am in terrible trouble, greater than I can well express—"

Poirot waved his hand. "I comprehend your anxiety. Mademoiselle Saintclair is a very dear friend, is it not so?"

The prince replied simply: "I hope to make her my wife."

Poirot sat up in his chair, and his eyes opened.

The prince continued: "I should not be the first of my family to make a morganatic marriage. My brother Alexander has also defied the Emperor. We are living now in more enlightened days, free from the old caste-prejudice. Besides, Mademoiselle Saintclair, in actual fact, is quite my equal in rank. You have heard hints as to her history?"

"There are many romantic stories of her origin— not an uncommon thing with famous dancers. I have heard that she is the daughter of an Irish charwoman, also the story which makes her mother a Russian grand duchess."

"The first story is, of course, nonsense," said the young man. "But the second is true. Valerie, though bound to secrecy, has let me guess as much. Besides, she proves it unconsciously in a thousand ways. I believe in heredity, M. Poirot."

"I too believe in heredity," said Poirot thoughtfully. "I have seen some strange things in connection with it—*moi qui vous parle* . . . But to business, *M. le Prince*. What do you want of me? What do you fear? I may speak freely, may I not? Is there anything to connect Mademoiselle Saintclair with the crime? She knew Reedburn of course?"

"Yes. He professed to be in love with her."

"And she?"

"She would have nothing to say to him."

Poirot looked at him keenly. "Had she any reason to fear him?"

The young man hesitated. "There was an incident. You know Zara, the clairvoyant?"

"No."

"She is wonderful. You should consult her some time. Valerie and I went to see her last week. She read the cards for us. She spoke to Valerie of trouble—of gathering clouds; then she turned up the last card—the covering card, they call it. It was the king of clubs. She said to Valerie: 'Beware. There is a man who holds you in his power. You fear him—you are in great danger through him. You know whom I mean?' Valerie was white to the lips. She nodded and said: 'Yes, yes, I know.' Shortly afterwards we left. Zara's last words to Valerie were: 'Beware of the king of clubs. Danger threatens you!' I questioned Valerie. She would tell me nothing—assured me that all was well. But now, after last night, I am more sure than ever that in the king of clubs Valerie saw Reedburn, and that he was the man she feared."

The Prince paused abruptly. "Now you understand my agitation when I opened the paper this morning. Supposing Valerie, in a fit of madness—oh, it is impossible!"

Poirot rose from his seat, and patted the young man kindly on the shoulder. "Do not distress yourself, I beg of you. Leave it in my hands."

"You will go to Streatham? I gather she is still there, at Daisymead—prostrated by the shock."

"I will go at once."

"I have arranged matters—through the embassy. You will be allowed access everywhere."

"Then we will depart—Hastings, you will accompany me? *Au revoir, M. le Prince.*"

II

Mon Désir was an exceptionally fine villa, thoroughly modern and comfortable. A short carriage-drive led up to it from the road, and beautiful gardens extended behind the house for some acres.

On mentioning Prince Paul's name, the butler who answered the door at once took us to the scene of the tragedy. The library was a magnificent room, running from back to front of the whole building, with a window at either end, one giving on the front carriage-drive, and the other on the garden. It was in the recess of the latter that the body had lain. It had been removed not long before, the police having concluded their examination.

"That is annoying," I murmured to Poirot. "Who knows what clues they may have destroyed?"

My little friend smiled. "Eh—Eh! How often must I tell you that clues come from *within?* In the little grey cells of the brain lies the solution of every mystery."

He turned to the butler. "I suppose, except for the removal of the body, the room has not been touched?"

"No, sir. It's just as it was when the police came up last night."

"These curtains, now. I see they pull right across the window recess. They are the same in the other window. Were they drawn last night?"

"Yes, sir, I draw them every night."

"Then Reedburn must have drawn them back himself?"

"I suppose so, sir."

"Did you know your master expected a visitor last night?"

"He did not say so, sir. But he gave orders he was not to be disturbed after dinner. You see, sir, there is a door leading out of the library on to the terrace at the side of the house. He could have admitted anyone that way."

"Was he in the habit of doing that?"

The butler coughed discreetly. "I believe so, sir."

Poirot strode to the door in question. It was unlocked. He stepped through it on to the terrace which joined the drive on the right; on the left it led up to a red brick wall.

"The fruit garden, sir. There is a door leading into it farther along, but it was always locked at six o'clock."

Poirot nodded, and reentered the library, the butler following.

"Did you hear nothing of last night's events?"

"Well, sir, we heard voices in the library, a little before nine. But that wasn't unusual, especially being a lady's voice. But of course, once we were all in the servants' hall, right the other side, we didn't hear anything at all. And then, about eleven o'clock, the police came."

"How many voices did you hear?"

"I couldn't say, sir. I only noticed the lady's."

"Ah!"

"I beg pardon, sir, but Dr. Ryan is still in the house, if you would care to see him."

We jumped at the suggestion, and in a few

minutes the doctor, a cheery, middle-aged man, joined us, and gave Poirot all the information he required. Reedburn had been lying near the window, his head by the marble window seat. There were two wounds, one between the eyes, and the other, the fatal one, on the back of the head.

"He was lying on his back?"

"Yes. There is the mark." He pointed to a small dark stain on the floor.

"Could not the blow on the back of the head have been caused by his striking the floor?"

"Impossible. Whatever the weapon was, it penetrated some distance into the skull."

Poirot looked thoughtfully in front of him. In the embrasure of each window was a carved marble seat, the arms being fashioned in the form of a lion's head. A light came into Poirot's eyes. "Supposing he had fallen backwards on this projecting lion's head, and slipped from there to the ground. Would not that cause a wound such as you describe?"

"Yes, it would. But the angle at which he was lying makes that theory impossible. And besides there could not fail to be traces of blood on the marble of the seat."

"Unless they were washed away?"

The doctor shrugged his shoulders. "That is hardly likely. It would be to no one's advantage to give an accident the appearance of murder."

"Quite so," acquiesced Poirot. "Could either of the blows have been struck by a woman, do you think?"

"Oh, quite out of the question, I should say. You are thinking of Mademoiselle Saintclair, I suppose?"

"I think of no one in particular until I am sure," said Poirot gently.

He turned his attention to the open french window, and the doctor continued:

"It is through here that Mademoiselle Saintclair fled. You can just catch a glimpse of Daisymead between the trees. Of course, there are many houses nearer to the front of the house on the road, but as it happens, Daisymead, though some distance away, is the only house visible this side."

"Thank you for your amiability, Doctor," said Poirot. "Come, Hastings, we will follow the footsteps of Mademoiselle."

III

Poirot led the way down through the garden, out through an iron gate, across a short stretch of green and in through the garden gate of Daisymead, which was an unpretentious little house in about half an acre of ground. There was a small flight of steps leading up to a french window. Poirot nodded in their direction.

"That is the way Mademoiselle Saintclair went.

For us, who have not her urgency to plead, it will be better to go round to the front door."

A maid admitted us and took us into the drawing room, then went in search of Mrs. Oglander. The room had evidently not been touched since the night before. The ashes were still in the grate, and the bridge table was still in the centre of the room, with a dummy exposed, and the hands thrown down. The place was somewhat overloaded with gimcrack ornaments, and a good many family portraits of surpassing ugliness adorned the walls.

Poirot gazed at them more leniently than I did, and straightened one or two that were hanging a shade askew. "*La famille*, it is a strong tie, is it not? Sentiment, it takes the place of beauty."

I agreed, my eyes being fixed on a family group comprising a gentleman with whiskers, a lady with a high "front" of hair, a solid, thick-set boy, and two little girls tied up with a good many unnecessary bows of ribbon. I took this to be the Oglander family in earlier days, and studied it with interest.

The door opened, and a young woman came in. Her dark hair was neatly arranged, and she wore a drab-coloured sportscoat and a tweed skirt.

She looked at us inquiringly. Poirot stepped forward. "Miss Oglander? I regret to derange you—especially after all you have been through. The whole affair must have been most disturbing."

"It has been rather upsetting," admitted the young lady cautiously. I began to think that the elements of drama were wasted on Miss Oglander, that her lack of imagination rose superior to any tragedy. I was confirmed in this belief as she continued: "I must apologize for the state this room is in. Servants get so foolishly excited."

"It was here that you were sitting last night, *n'est-ce pas?*"

"Yes, we were playing bridge after supper, when—"

"Excuse me—how long had you been playing?"

"Well—" Miss Oglander considered. "I really can't say. I suppose it must have been about ten o'clock. We had had several rubbers, I know."

"And you yourself were sitting—where?"

"Facing the window. I was playing with my mother and had gone one no trump. Suddenly, without any warning, the window burst open, and Miss Saintclair staggered into the room."

"You recognized her?"

"I had a vague idea her face was familiar."

"She is still here, is she not?"

"Yes, but she refuses to see anyone. She is still quite prostrated."

"I think she will see me. Will you tell her that I am here at the express request of Prince Paul of Maurania?"

I fancied that the mention of a royal prince rather shook Miss Oglander's imperturbable calm. But she left the room on her errand without any further remark, and returned almost immediately to say that Mademoiselle Saintclair would see us in her room.

We followed her upstairs, and into a fair-sized light bedroom. On a couch by the window a woman was lying who turned her head as we entered. The contrast between the two women struck me at once, the more so as in actual features and colouring they were not unalike—but oh, the difference! Not a look, not a gesture of Valerie Saintclair's but expressed drama. She seemed to exhale an atmosphere of romance. A scarlet flannel dressing gown covered her feet—a homely garment in all conscience; but the charm of her personality invested it with an exotic flavour, and it seemed an Eastern robe of glowing colour.

Her large dark eyes fastened themselves on Poirot.

"You come from Paul?" Her voice matched her appearance—it was full and languid.

"Yes, mademoiselle. I am here to serve him—and you."

"What do you want to know?"

"Everything that happened last night. *But everything!*"

She smiled rather wearily.

"Do you think I should lie? I am not stupid. I see well enough that there can be no concealment. He held a secret of mine, that man who is dead. He threatened me with it. For Paul's sake, I endeavoured to make terms with him. I could not risk losing Paul . . . Now that he is dead, I am safe. But for all that, I did not kill him."

Poirot shook his head with a smile. "It is not necessary to tell me that, mademoiselle. Now recount to me what happened last night."

"I offered him money. He appeared to be willing to treat with me. He appointed last night at nine o'clock. I was to go to Mon Désir. I knew the place; I had been there before. I was to go round to the side door into the library, so that the servants should not see me."

"Excuse me, mademoiselle, but were you not afraid to trust yourself alone there at night?"

Was it my fancy, or was there a momentary pause before she answered?

"Perhaps I was. But you see, there was no one I could ask to go with me. And I was desperate. Reedburn admitted me to the library. Oh, that man! I am glad he is dead! He played with me, as a cat does with a mouse. He taunted me. I begged and implored him on my knees. I offered him every jewel I have. All in vain! Then he named his own terms. Perhaps you can guess what they were. I refused. I told him what I thought of him. I raved at him. He remained calmly smiling. And then, as I fell to silence at last, there was a sound— from behind the curtain in the window . . . He heard it too. He strode to the curtains and flung them wide apart. There was a man there, hiding— a dreadful-looking man, a sort of tramp. He struck at Mr. Reedburn—then he struck again, and he went down. The tramp clutched at me with his bloodstained hand. I tore myself free, slipped through the window, and ran for my life. Then I perceived the lights in this house, and made for them. The blinds were up, and I saw some people playing bridge. I almost fell into the room. I just managed to gasp out 'Murder!' and then everything went black—"

"Thank you, mademoiselle. It must have been a great shock to your nervous system. As to this tramp, could you describe him? Do you remember what he was wearing?"

"No—it was all so quick. But I should know the man anywhere. His face is burnt in on my brain."

"Just one more question, mademoiselle. The curtains of the *other* window, the one giving on the drive, were they drawn?"

For the first time a puzzled expression crept over the dancer's face. She seemed to be trying to remember.

"*Eh bien, mademoiselle?*"

"I think—I am almost sure—yes, quite sure! They were *not* drawn."

"That is curious, since the other ones were. No matter. It is, I dare say, of no great importance. You are remaining here long, mademoiselle?"

"The doctor thinks I shall be fit to return to town tomorrow." She looked round the room. Miss Oglander had gone out. "These people, they are very kind—but they are not of my world. I shock them! And to me—well, I am not fond of the *bourgeoisie*!"

A faint note of bitterness underlay her words.

Poirot nodded. "I understand. I hope I have not fatigued you unduly with my questions?"

"Not at all, monsieur. I am only too anxious Paul should know all as soon as possible."

"Then I will wish you good day, mademoiselle."

As Poirot was leaving the room, he paused, and pounced on a pair of patent-leather slippers. "Yours, mademoiselle?"

"Yes, monsieur. They have just been cleaned and brought up."

"Ah!" said Poirot, as we descended the stairs. "It seems that the domestics are not too excited to clean shoes, though they forget a grate. Well, *mon ami*, at first there appeared to be one or two points of interest, but I fear, I very much fear, that we must regard the case as finished. It all seems straightforward enough."

"And the murderer?"

"Hercule Poirot does not hunt down tramps," replied my friend grandiloquently.

IV

Miss Oglander met us in the hall. "If you will wait in the drawing room a minute, Mamma would like to speak to you."

The room was still untouched, and Poirot idly gathered up the cards, shuffling them with his tiny, fastidiously groomed hands.

"Do you know what I think, my friend?"

"No?" I said eagerly.

"I think that Miss Oglander made a mistake in going one no trump. She should have gone three spades."

"Poirot! You are the limit."

"*Mon Dieu*, I cannot always be talking blood and thunder!"

Suddenly he stiffened: "Hastings—*Hastings*. See! The king of clubs is missing from the pack!"

"Zara!" I cried.

"Eh?" he did not seem to understand my allusion. Mechanically he stacked the cards and put them away in their cases. His face was very grave.

"Hastings," he said at last, "I, Hercule Poirot, have come near to making a big mistake—a very big mistake."

I gazed at him, impressed, but utterly uncomprehending.

"We must begin again, Hastings. Yes, we must begin again. But this time we shall not err."

He was interrupted by the entrance of a handsome middle-aged lady. She carried some household books in her hand. Poirot bowed to her.

"Do I understand, sir, that you are a friend of— er—Miss Saintclair's?"

"I come from a friend of hers, madame."

"Oh, I see. I thought perhaps—"

Poirot suddenly waved brusquely at the window.

"Your blinds were not pulled down last night?"

"No—I suppose that is why Miss Saintclair saw the light so plainly."

"There was moonlight last night. I wonder that you did not see Mademoiselle Saintclair from your seat here facing the windows?"

"I suppose we were engrossed with our game. Nothing like this has ever happened before to us."

"I can quite believe that, madame. And I will put your mind at rest. Mademoiselle Saintclair is leaving tomorrow."

"Oh!" The good lady's face cleared.

"And I will wish you good morning, madame."

A servant was cleaning the steps as we went out of the front door. Poirot addressed her.

"Was it you who cleaned the shoes of the young lady upstairs?"

The maid shook her head. "No, sir. I don't think they've been cleaned."

"Who cleaned them, then?" I inquired of Poirot, as we walked down the road.

"Nobody. They did not need cleaning."

"I grant that walking on the road or path on a fine night would not soil them. But surely after going through the long grass of the garden, they would have been soiled and stained."

"Yes," said Poirot with a curious smile. "In that case, I agree, they would have been stained."

"But—"

"Have patience a little half hour, my friend. We are going back to Mon Désir."

V

The butler looked surprised at our reappearance, but offered no objection to our returning to the library.

"Hi, that's the wrong window, Poirot," I cried as he made for the one overlooking the carriage-drive.

"I think not, my friend. See here." He pointed to the marble lion's head. On it was a faint dis-coloured smear. He shifted his finger and pointed to a similar stain on the polished floor.

"Someone struck Reedburn a blow with his clenched fist between the eyes. He fell backward on this projecting bit of marble, then slipped to the floor. Afterwards, he was dragged across the floor to the other window, and laid there instead, but not quite at the same angle, as the Doctor's evidence told us."

"But why? It seems utterly unnecessary."

"On the contrary, it was essential. Also, it is the key to the murderer's identity—though, by the way, he had no intention of killing Reedburn, and so it is hardly permissible to call him a murderer. He must be a very strong man!"

"Because of having dragged the body across the floor?"

"Not altogether. It has been an interesting case. I nearly made an imbecile of myself, though."

"Do you mean to say it is over, that you know everything?"

"Yes."

A remembrance smote me. "No," I cried. "There is one thing you do *not* know!"

"And that?"

"You do not know where the missing king of clubs is!"

"Eh? Oh, that is droll! That is very droll, my friend."

"Why?"

"Because it is in my pocket!" He drew it forth with a flourish.

"Oh!" I said, rather crestfallen. "Where did you find it? Here?"

"There was nothing sensational about it. It had simply not been taken out with the other cards. It was in the box."

"H'm! All the same, it gave you an idea, didn't it?"

"Yes, my friend. I present my respects to His Majesty."

"And to Madame Zara!"

"Ah, yes—to the lady also."

"Well, what are we going to do now?"

"We are going to return to town. But I must have a few words with a certain lady at Daisymead first."

The same little maid opened the door to us.

"They're all at lunch now, sir—unless it's Miss Saintclair you want to see, and she's resting."

"It will do if I can see Mrs. Oglander for a few minutes. Will you tell her?"

We were led into the drawing room to wait. I had a glimpse of the family in the dining room as we passed, now reinforced by the presence of two heavy, solid-looking men, one with a moustache, the other with a beard also.

In a few minutes Mrs. Oglander came into the room, looking inquiringly at Poirot, who bowed.

"Madame, we, in our country, have a great tenderness, a great respect for the mother. The *mère de famille*, she is everything!"

Mrs. Oglander looked rather astonished at this opening.

"It is for that reason that I have come—to allay a mother's anxiety. The murderer of Mr. Reedburn will not be discovered. Have no fear. I, Hercule Poirot, tell you so. I am right, am I not? Or is it a wife that I must reassure?"

There was a moment's pause. Mrs. Oglander seemed searching Poirot with her eyes. At last she said quietly: "I don't know how you know—but yes, you are right."

Poirot nodded gravely. "That is all, madame. But do not be uneasy. Your English policemen have not the eyes of Hercule Poirot." He tapped the family portrait on the wall with his fingernail.

"You had another daughter once. She is dead, madame?"

Again there was a pause, as she searched him with her eyes. Then she answered: "Yes, she is dead."

"Ah!" said Poirot briskly. "Well, we must return to town. You permit that I return the king of clubs to the pack? It was your only slip. You understand, to have played bridge for an hour or so, with only fifty-one cards—well, no one who knows anything of the game would credit it for a minute! *Bonjour*!"

"And now, my friend," said Poirot as we stepped towards the station, "you see it all!"

"I see nothing! Who killed Reedburn?"

"John Oglander, Junior. I was not quite sure if it was the father or the son, but I fixed on the son as being the stronger and younger of the two. It had to be one of them, because of the window."

"Why?"

"There were four exits from the library—two doors, two windows; but evidently only one would do. Three exits gave on the front, directly or indirectly. The tragedy had to occur in the back window in order to make it appear that Valerie Saintclair came to Daisymead by chance. Really, of course, she fainted, and John Oglander carried her across over his shoulders. That is why I said he must be a strong man."

"Did they go there together, then?"

"Yes. You remember Valerie's hesitation when I asked her if she was not afraid to go alone? John Oglander went with her—which didn't improve Reedburn's temper, I fancy. They quarrelled, and it was probably some insult levelled at Valerie that made Oglander hit him. The rest, you know."

"But why the bridge?"

"Bridge presupposes four players. A simple thing like that carries a lot of conviction. Who would have supposed that there had been only three people in that room all the evening?"

I was still puzzled.

"There's one thing I don't understand. What have the Oglanders to do with the dancer Valerie Saintclair?"

"Ah, that I wonder you did not see. And yet you looked long enough at that picture on the wall—longer than I did. Mrs. Oglander's other daughter may be dead to her family, but the world knows her as Valerie Saintclair!"

"What?"

"Did you not see the resemblance the moment you saw the two sisters together?"

"No," I confessed. "I only thought how extraordinarily dissimilar they were."

"That is because your mind is so open to external romantic impressions, my dear Hastings. The features are almost identical. So is the colouring. The interesting thing is that Valerie is ashamed of her family, and her family is ashamed of her. Nevertheless, in a moment of peril, she turned to her brother for help, and when things went wrong, they all hung together in a remarkable way. Family strength is a marvellous thing. They can all act, that family. That is where Valerie gets her histrionic talent from. I, like Prince Paul, believe in heredity! They deceived *me!* But for a lucky accident, and test question to Mrs. Oglander by which I got her to contradict her daughter's account of how they were sitting, the Oglander family would have put a defeat on Hercule Poirot."

"What shall you tell the Prince?"

"That Valerie could not possibly have committed the crime, and that I doubt if that tramp will ever be found. Also, to convey my compliments to Zara. A curious coincidence, that! I think I shall call this little affair the Adventure of the King of Clubs. What do you think, my friend?"

Eight

THE SUBMARINE PLANS

I

A note had been brought by special messenger. Poirot read it, and a gleam of excitement and interest came into his eyes as he did so. He dismissed the man with a few curt words and then turned to me.

"Pack a bag with all haste, my friend. We're going down to Sharples."

I started at the mention of the famous country place of Lord Alloway. Head of the newly formed Ministry of Defence, Lord Alloway was a prominent member of the Cabinet. As Sir Ralph Curtis, head of a great engineering firm, he had made his mark in the House of Commons, and he was now freely spoken of as *the* coming man, and the one most likely to be asked to form a ministry should the rumours as to Mr. David MacAdam's health prove well founded.

A big Rolls-Royce car was waiting for us below, and as we glided off into the darkness, I plied Poirot with questions.

"What on earth can they want us for at this time of night?" I demanded. It was past eleven.

Poirot shook his head. "Something of the most urgent, without doubt."

"I remember," I said, "that some years ago there was some rather ugly scandal about Ralph Curtis, as he then was—some jugglery with shares, I believe. In the end, he was completely exonerated; but perhaps something of the kind has arisen again?"

"It would hardly be necessary for him to send for me in the middle of the night, my friend."

I was forced to agree, and the remainder of the journey was passed in silence. Once out of London, the powerful car forged rapidly ahead, and we arrived at Sharples in a little under the hour.

A pontifical butler conducted us at once to a small study where Lord Alloway was awaiting us. He sprang up to greet us—a tall, spare man who seemed actually to radiate power and vitality.

"M. Poirot, I am delighted to see you. It is the second time the government has demanded your services. I remember only too well what you did for us during the war, when the Prime Minister was kidnapped in that astounding fashion. Your masterly deductions—and may I add, your discretion?—saved the situation."

Poirot's eyes twinkled a little.

"Do I gather then, milor', that this is another case for—discretion?"

"Most emphatically. Sir Harry and I—oh, let

me introduce you—Admiral Sir Harry Weardale, our First Sea Lord—M. Poirot and—let me see, Captain—"

"Hastings," I supplied.

"I've often heard of you, M. Poirot," said Sir Harry, shaking hands. "This is a most unaccountable business, and if you can solve it, we'll be extremely grateful to you."

I liked the First Sea Lord immediately, a square, bluff sailor of the good old-fashioned type.

Poirot looked inquiringly at them both, and Alloway took up the tale.

"Of course, you understand that all this is in confidence, M. Poirot. We have had a most serious loss. The plans of the new Z type of submarine have been stolen."

"When was that?"

"Tonight—less than three hours ago. You can appreciate perhaps, M. Poirot, the magnitude of the disaster. It is essential that the loss should not be made public. I will give you the facts as briefly as possible. My guests over the weekend were the Admiral, here, his wife and son, and Mrs. Conrad, a lady well known in London society. The ladies retired to bed early—about ten o'clock; so did Mr. Leonard Weardale. Sir Harry is down here partly for the purpose of discussing the construction of this new type of submarine with me. Accordingly, I asked Mr. Fitzroy, my secretary, to get out the plans from the safe in the corner there, and to arrange them ready for me, as well as various other documents that bore upon the subject in hand. While he was doing this, the Admiral and I strolled up and down the terrace, smoking cigars and enjoying the warm June air. We finished our smoke and our chat, and decided to get down to business. Just as we turned at the far end of the terrace, I fancied I saw a shadow slip out of the french window here, cross the terrace, and disappear. I paid very little attention, however. I knew Fitzroy to be in this room, and it never entered my head that anything might be amiss. There, of course, I am to blame. Well, we retraced our steps along the terrace and entered this room by the window just as Fitzroy entered it from the hall.

" 'Got everything out we are likely to need, Fitzroy?' I asked.

" 'I think so, Lord Alloway. The papers are all on your desk,' he answered. And then he wished us both good night.

" 'Just wait a minute,' I said, going to the desk. 'I may want something I haven't mentioned.'

"I looked quickly through the papers that were lying there.

" 'You've forgotten the most important of the lot, Fitzroy,' I said. 'The actual plans of the submarine!'

" 'The plans are right on top, Lord Alloway.'

" 'Oh no, they're not,' I said, turning over the papers.

" 'But I put them there not a minute ago!'

" 'Well, they're not here now,' I said.

"Fitzroy advanced with a bewildered expression on his face. The thing seemed incredible. We turned over the papers on the desk; we hunted through the safe; but at last we had to make up our minds to it that the papers were gone—and gone within the short space of about three minutes while Fitzroy was absent from the room."

"Why did he leave the room?" asked Poirot quickly.

"Just what I asked him," exclaimed Sir Harry.

"It appears," said Lord Alloway, "that just when he had finished arranging the papers on my desk, he was startled by hearing a woman scream. He dashed out into the hall. On the stairs he discovered Mrs. Conrad's French maid. The girl looked very white and upset, and declared that she had seen a ghost—a tall figure dressed all in white that moved without a sound. Fitzroy laughed at her fears and told her, in more or less polite language, not to be a fool. Then he returned to this room just as we entered from the window."

"It all seems very clear," said Poirot thoughtfully. "The only question is, was the maid an accomplice? Did she scream by arrangement with her confederate lurking outside, or was he merely waiting there in the hope of an opportunity presenting itself? It was a man, I suppose—not a woman you saw?"

"I can't tell you, M. Poirot. It was just a—shadow."

The admiral gave such a peculiar snort that it could not fail to attract attention.

"M. l'Amiral has something to say, I think," said Poirot quietly, with a slight smile. "You saw this shadow, Sir Harry?"

"No, I didn't," returned the other. "And neither did Alloway. The branch of a tree flapped, or something, and then afterwards, when we discovered the theft, he leaped to the conclusion that he had seen someone pass across the terrace. His imagination played a trick on him; that's all."

"I am not usually credited with having much imagination," said Lord Alloway with a slight smile.

"Nonsense, we've all got imagination. We can all work ourselves up to believe that we've seen more than we have. I've had a lifetime of experience at sea, and I'll back my eyes against those of any landsman. I was looking right down the terrace, and I'd have seen the same if there was anything to see."

He was quite excited over the matter. Poirot rose and stepped quickly to the window.

"You permit?" he asked. "We must settle this point if possible."

He went out upon the terrace, and we followed him. He had taken an electric torch from his pocket, and was playing the light along the edge of the grass that bordered the terrace.

"Where did he cross the terrace, milor'?" he asked.

"About opposite the window, I should say."

Poirot continued to play the torch for some minutes longer, walking the entire length of the terrace and back. Then he shut it off and straightened himself up.

"Sir Harry is right—and you are wrong, milor'," he said quietly. "It rained heavily earlier this evening. Anyone who passed over that grass could not avoid leaving footmarks. But there are none—none at all."

His eyes went from one man's face to the other's. Lord Alloway looked bewildered and unconvinced; the Admiral expressed a noisy gratification.

"Knew I couldn't be wrong," he declared. "Trust my eyes anywhere."

He was such a picture of an honest old sea-dog that I could not help smiling.

"So that brings us to the people in the house," said Poirot smoothly. "Let us come inside again. Now, milor', while Mr. Fitzroy was speaking to the maid on the stairs, could anyone have seized the opportunity to enter the study from the hall?"

Lord Alloway shook his head.

"Quite impossible—they would have had to pass him in order to do so."

"And Mr. Fitzroy himself—you are sure of him, eh?"

Lord Alloway flushed.

"Absolutely, M. Poirot. I will answer confidently for my secretary. It is quite impossible that he should be concerned in the matter in any way."

"Everything seems to be impossible," remarked Poirot rather drily. "Possibly the plans attached to themselves a little pair of wings, and flew away—*comme ça!*" He blew his lips out like a comical cherub.

"The whole thing is impossible," declared Lord Alloway impatiently. "But I beg, M. Poirot, that you will not dream of suspecting Fitzroy. Consider for one moment—had he wished to take the plans, what could have been easier for him than to take a tracing of them without going to the trouble of stealing them?"

"There, milor'," said Poirot with approval, "you make a remark *bien juste*—I see that you have a mind orderly and methodical. *L'Angleterre* is happy in possessing you."

Lord Alloway looked rather embarrassed by this sudden burst of praise. Poirot returned to the matter in hand.

"The room in which you had been sitting all the evening—"

"The drawing room? Yes?"

"That also has a window on the terrace, since I remember your saying you went out that way. Would it not be possible for someone to come out by the drawing room window and in by this one while Mr. Fitzroy was out of the room, and return the same way?"

"But we'd have seen them," objected the Admiral.

"Not if you had your backs turned, walking the other way."

"Fitzroy was only out of the room a few minutes, the time it would take us to walk to the end and back."

"No matter—it is a possibility—in fact, the only one as things stand."

"But there was no one in the drawing room when we went out," said the Admiral.

"They may have come there afterwards."

"You mean," said Lord Alloway slowly, "that when Fitzroy heard the maid scream and went out, someone was already concealed in the drawing room, and that they darted in and out through the windows, and only left the drawing room when Fitzroy had returned to this room?"

"The methodical mind again," said Poirot, bowing.

"You express the matter perfectly."

"One of the servants, perhaps?"

"Or a guest. It was Mrs. Conrad's maid who

screamed. What exactly can you tell me of Mrs. Conrad?"

Lord Alloway considered for a minute.

"I told you that she is a lady well known in society. That is true in the sense that she gives large parties, and goes everywhere. But very little is known as to where she really comes from, and what her past life has been. She is a lady who frequents diplomatic and Foreign Office circles as much as possible. The Secret Service is inclined to ask—why?"

"I see," said Poirot. "And she was asked here this weekend—"

"So that—shall we say?—we might observe her at close quarters."

"*Parfaitement*! It is possible that she has turned the tables on you rather neatly."

Lord Alloway looked discomfited, and Poirot continued: "Tell me, milor', was any reference made in her hearing to the subjects you and the Admiral were going to discuss together?"

"Yes," admitted the other. "Sir Harry said: 'And now for our submarine! To work!' or something of that sort. The others had left the room, but she had come back for a book."

"I see," said Poirot thoughtfully. "Milor', it is very late—but this is an urgent affair. I would like to question the members of this house party at once if it is possible."

"It can be managed, of course," said Lord

Alloway. "The awkward thing is, we don't want to let it get about more than can be helped. Of course, Lady Juliet Weardale and young Leonard are all right—but Mrs. Conrad, if she is not guilty, is rather a different proposition. Perhaps you could just state that an important paper is missing, without specifying what it is, or going into any of the circumstances of the disappearance?"

"Exactly what I was about to propose myself," said Poirot, beaming. "In fact, in all three cases. Monsieur the Admiral will pardon me, but even the best of wives—"

"No offence," said Sir Harry. "All women talk, bless 'em! I wish Juliet would talk a little more and play bridge a little less. But women are like that nowadays, never happy unless they're dancing or gambling. I'll get Juliet and Leonard up, shall I, Alloway?"

"Thank you. I'll call the French maid. M. Poirot will want to see her, and she can rouse her mistress. I'll attend to it now. In the meantime, I'll send Fitzroy along."

II

Mr. Fitzroy was a pale, thin young man with pince-nez and a frigid expression. His statement was practically word for word what Lord Alloway had already told us.

"What is your own theory, Mr. Fitzroy?"

Mr. Fitzroy shrugged his shoulders.

"Undoubtedly someone who knew the hang of things was waiting his chance outside. He could see what went on through the window, and he slipped in when I left the room. It's a pity Lord Alloway didn't give chase then and there when he saw the fellow leave."

Poirot did not undeceive him. Instead he asked: "Do you believe the story of the French maid—that she had seen a ghost?"

"Well, hardly, M. Poirot!"

"I mean—that she really thought so?"

"Oh, as to that, I can't say. She certainly seemed rather upset. She had her hands to her head."

"Aha!" cried Poirot with the air of one who has made a discovery. "Is that so indeed—and she was without doubt a pretty girl?"

"I didn't notice particularly," said Mr. Fitzroy in a repressive voice.

"You did not see her mistress, I suppose?"

"As a matter of fact, I did. She was in the gallery at the top of the steps and was calling her—'Léonie!' Then she saw me—and of course retired."

"Upstairs," said Poirot, frowning.

"Of course, I realize that all this is very unpleasant for me—or rather would have been, if Lord Alloway had not chanced to see the man actually leaving. In any case, I should be glad if

248

you would make a point of searching my room—and myself."

"You really wish that?"

"Certainly I do."

What Poirot would have replied I do not know, but at that moment Lord Alloway reappeared and informed us that the two ladies and Mr. Leonard Weardale were in the drawing room.

The women were in becoming negligees. Mrs. Conrad was a beautiful woman of thirty-five, with golden hair and a slight tendency to *embonpoint*. Lady Juliet Weardale must have been forty, tall and dark, very thin, still beautiful, with exquisite hands and feet, and a restless, haggard manner. Her son was rather an effeminate-looking young man, as great a contrast to his bluff, hearty father as could well be imagined.

Poirot gave forth the little rigmarole we had agreed upon, and then explained that he was anxious to know if anyone had heard or seen anything that night which might assist us.

Turning to Mrs. Conrad first, he asked her if she would be so kind as to inform him exactly what her movements had been.

"Let me see . . . I went upstairs. I rang for my maid. Then, as she did not put in an appearance, I came out and called her. I could hear her talking on the stairs. After she had brushed my hair, I sent her away—she was in a very curious nervous state. I read awhile and then went to bed."

"And you, Lady Juliet?"

"I went straight upstairs and to bed. I was very tired."

"What about your book, dear?" asked Mrs. Conrad with a sweet smile.

"My book?" Lady Juliet flushed.

"Yes, you know, when I sent Léonie away, you were coming up the stairs. You had been down to the drawing room for a book, you said."

"Oh yes, I did go down. I—I forgot."

Lady Juliet clasped her hands nervously together.

"Did you hear Mrs. Conrad's maid scream, milady?"

"No—no, I didn't."

"How curious—because you must have been in the drawing room at the time."

"I heard nothing," said Lady Juliet in a firmer voice.

Poirot turned to young Leonard.

"Monsieur?"

"Nothing doing. I went straight upstairs and turned in."

Poirot stroked his chin.

"Alas, I fear there is nothing to help me here. Mesdames and monsieur, I regret—I regret infinitely to have deranged you from your slumbers for so little. Accept my apologies, I pray of you."

Gesticulating and apologizing, he marshalled

them out. He returned with the French maid, a pretty, impudent-looking girl. Alloway and Weardale had gone out with the ladies.

"Now, mademoiselle," said Poirot in a brisk tone, "let us have the truth. Recount to me no histories. Why did you scream on the stairs?"

"Ah, monsieur, I saw a tall figure—all in white—"

Poirot arrested her with an energetic shake of his forefinger.

"Did I not say, recount to me no histories? I will make a guess. He kissed you, did he not? M. Leonard Weardale, I mean?"

"*Eh bien, monsieur*, and after all, what is a kiss?"

"Under the circumstances, it is most natural," replied Poirot gallantly. "I myself, or Hastings here—but tell me just what occurred."

"He came up behind me, and caught me. I was startled, and I screamed. If I had known, I would not have screamed—but he came upon me like a cat. Then came *M. le secrêtaire*. M. Leonard flew up the stairs. And what could I say? Especially to a *jeune homme comme ça—tellement comme il faut*? *Ma foi*, I invent a ghost."

"And all is explained," cried Poirot genially. "You then mounted to the chamber of Madame your mistress. Which is her room, by the way?"

"It is at the end, monsieur. That way."

251

"Directly over the study, then. *Bien*, mademoiselle, I will detain you no longer. And *la prochaine fois*, do not scream."

Handing her out, he came back to me with a smile.

"An interesting case, is it not, Hastings? I begin to have a few little ideas. *Et vous*?"

"What was Leonard Weardale doing on the stairs? I don't like that young man, Poirot. He's a thorough young rake, I should say."

"I agree with you, *mon ami*."

"Fitzroy seems an honest fellow."

"Lord Alloway is certainly insistent on that point."

"And yet there is something in his manner—"

"That is almost too good to be true? I felt it myself. On the other hand, our friend Mrs. Conrad is certainly no good at all."

"And her room is over the study," I said musingly, and keeping a sharp eye on Poirot.

He shook his head with a slight smile.

"No, *mon ami*, I cannot bring myself seriously to believe that that immaculate lady swarmed down the chimney, or let herself down from the balcony."

As he spoke, the door opened, and to my great surprise, Lady Juliet Weardale flitted in.

"M. Poirot," she said somewhat breathlessly, "can I speak to you alone?"

"Milady, Captain Hastings is as my other self.

252

You can speak before him as though he were a thing of no account, not there at all. Be seated, I pray you."

She sat down, still keeping her eyes fixed on Poirot.

"What I have to say is—rather difficult. You are in charge of this case. If the—papers were to be returned, would that end the matter? I mean, could it be done without questions being asked?"

Poirot stared hard at her.

"Let me understand you, madame. They are to be placed in my hand—is that right? And I am to return them to Lord Alloway on the condition that he asks no questions as to where I got them?"

She bowed her head. "That is what I mean. But I must be sure there will be no—publicity."

"I do not think Lord Alloway is particularly anxious for publicity," said Poirot grimly.

"You accept then?" she cried eagerly in response.

"A little moment, milady. It depends on how soon you can place those papers in my hands."

"Almost immediately."

Poirot glanced up at the clock.

"How soon, exactly?"

"Say—ten minutes," she whispered.

"I accept, milady."

She hurried from the room. I pursed my mouth up for a whistle.

"Can you sum up the situation for me, Hastings?"

"Bridge," I replied succinctly.

"Ah, you remember the careless words of Monsieur the Admiral! What a memory! I felicitate you, Hastings."

We said no more, for Lord Alloway came in, and looked inquiringly at Poirot.

"Have you any further ideas, M. Poirot? I am afraid the answers to your questions have been rather disappointing."

"Not at all, milor'. They have been quite sufficiently illuminating. It will be unnecessary for me to stay here any longer, and so, with your permission, I will return at once to London."

Lord Alloway seemed dumbfounded.

"But—but what have you discovered? Do you know who took the plans?"

"Yes, milor', I do. Tell me—in the case of the papers being returned to you anonymously, you would prosecute no further inquiry?"

Lord Alloway stared at him.

"Do you mean on payment of a sum of money?"

"No, milor', returned unconditionally."

"Of course, the recovery of the plans is the great thing," said Lord Alloway slowly. He looked puzzled and uncomprehending.

"Then I should seriously recommend you to adopt that course. Only you, the Admiral, and your secretary know of the loss. Only they need know of the restitution. And you may count on me to support you in every way—lay the mystery on my shoulders. You asked me to restore the papers—I have done so. You know no more." He rose and held out his hand. "Milor', I am glad to have met you. I have faith in you—and your devotion to England. You will guide her destinies with a strong, sure hand."

"M. Poirot—I swear to you that I will do my best. It may be a fault, or it may be a virtue—but I believe in myself."

"So does every great man. Me, I am the same!" said Poirot grandiloquently.

III

The car came round to the door in a few minutes, and Lord Alloway bade us farewell on the steps with renewed cordiality.

"That is a great man, Hastings," said Poirot as we drove off. "He has brains, resource, power. He is the strong man that England needs to guide her through these difficult days of reconstruction."

"I'm quite ready to agree with all you say, Poirot—but what about Lady Juliet? Is she to return the papers straight to Alloway? What will she think when she finds you have gone off without a word?"

"Hastings, I will ask you a little question. Why, when she was talking with me, did she not hand me the plans then and there?"

"She hadn't got them with her."

"Perfectly. How long would it take her to fetch

them from her room? Or from any hiding place in the house? You need not answer. I will tell you. Probably about two minutes and a half! Yet she asks for ten minutes. Why? Clearly she has to obtain them from some other person, and to reason or argue with that person before they give them up. Now, what person could that be? Not Mrs. Conrad, clearly, but a member of her own family, her husband or son. Which is it likely to be? Leonard Weardale said he went straight to bed. We know that to be untrue. Supposing his mother went to his room and found it empty; supposing she came down filled with a nameless dread—he is no beauty that son of hers! She does not find him, but later she hears him deny that he ever left his room. She leaps to the conclusion that he is the thief. Hence her interview with me.

"But, *mon ami*, we know something that Lady Juliet does not. We know that her son could not have been in the study, because he was on the stairs, making love to the pretty French maid. Although she does not know it, Leonard Weardale has an alibi."

"Well, then, who did steal the papers? We seem to have eliminated everybody—Lady Juliet, her son, Mrs. Conrad, the French maid—"

"Exactly. Use your little grey cells, my friend. The solution stares you in the face."

I shook my head blankly.

"But yes! If you would only persevere! See,

then, Fitzroy goes out of the study; he leaves the papers on the desk. A few minutes later Lord Alloway enters the room, goes to the desk, and the papers are gone. Only two things are possible: either Fitzroy did *not* leave the papers on the desk, but put them in his pocket—and that is not reasonable, because, as Alloway pointed out, he could have taken a tracing at his own convenience any time—or else the papers were still on the desk when Lord Alloway went to it—in which case they went into his pocket."

"Lord Alloway the thief," I said, dumbfounded. "But why? Why?"

"Did you not tell me of some scandal in the past? He was exonerated, you said. But suppose, after all, it had been true? In English public life there must be no scandal. If this were raked up and proved against him now—good-bye to his political career. We will suppose that he was being blackmailed, and the price asked was the submarine plans."

"But the man's a black traitor!" I cried.

"Oh no, he is not. He is clever and resourceful. Supposing, my friend, that he copied those plans, making—for he is a clever engineer—a slight alteration in each part which will render them quite impractible. He hands the faked plans to the enemy's agent—Mrs. Conrad, I fancy; but in order that no suspicion of their genuineness may arise, the plans must seem to be stolen. He does his best to throw no suspicion on anyone in the house, by pretending to see a man leaving the window. But there he ran up against the obstinacy of the Admiral. So his next anxiety is that no suspicion shall fall on Fitzroy."

"This is all guesswork on your part, Poirot," I objected.

"It is psychology, *mon ami*. A man who had handed over the real plans would not be overscrupulous as to who was likely to fall under suspicion. And why was he so anxious that no details of the robbery should be given to Mrs. Conrad? Because he had handed over the faked plans earlier in the evening, and did not want her to know that the theft could only have taken place later."

"I wonder if you are right," I said.

"Of course I am right. I spoke to Alloway as one great man to another—and he understood perfectly. You will see."

IV

One thing is quite certain. On the day when Lord Alloway became Prime Minister, a cheque and a signed photograph arrived; on the photograph were the words: *"To my discreet friend, Hercule Poirot—from Alloway."*

I believe that the Z type of submarine is causing great exultation in naval circles. They say it will revolutionize modern naval warfare. I have heard that a certain foreign power essayed to construct something of the same kind and the result was a dismal failure. But I still consider that Poirot was guessing. He will do it once too often one of these days.

Nine

The Adventure of
the Clapham Cook

I

At the time that I was sharing rooms with my friend Hercule Poirot, it was my custom to read aloud to him the headlines in the morning newspaper, the *Daily Blare.*

The *Daily Blare* was a paper that made the most of any opportunity for sensationalism. Robberies and murders did not lurk obscurely in its back pages. Instead they hit you in the eye in large type on the front page.

ABSCONDING BANK CLERK DISAPPEARS WITH FIFTY THOUSAND POUNDS' WORTH OF NEGOTIABLE SECURITIES, I read.

HUSBAND PUTS HIS HEAD IN GAS-OVEN. UNHAPPY HOME LIFE. MISSING TYPIST. PRETTY GIRL OF TWENTY-ONE. WHERE IS EDNA FIELD?

"There you are, Poirot, plenty to choose from. An absconding bank clerk, a mysterious suicide, a missing typist—which will you have?"

My friend was in a placid mood. He quietly shook his head.

"I am not greatly attracted to any of them, *mon ami*. Today I feel inclined for the life of ease. It would have to be a very interesting problem to tempt me from my chair. See you, I have affairs of importance of my own to attend to."

"Such as?"

"My wardrobe, Hastings. If I mistake not, there is on my new grey suit the spot of grease—only the unique spot, but it is sufficient to trouble me. Then there is my winter overcoat—I must lay him aside in the powder of Keatings. And I think—yes, I think—the moment is ripe for the trimmings of my moustaches—and afterwards I must apply the pomade."

"Well," I said, strolling to the window, "I doubt if you'll be able to carry out this delirious programme. That was a ring at the bell. You have a client."

"Unless the affair is one of national importance, I touch it not," declared Poirot with dignity.

A moment later our privacy was invaded by a stout red-faced lady who panted audibly as a result of her rapid ascent of the stairs.

"You're M. Poirot?" she demanded, as she sank into a chair.

"I am Hercule Poirot, yes, madame."

"You're not a bit like what I thought you'd be," said the lady, eyeing him with some disfavour.

"Did you pay for the bit in the paper saying what a clever detective you were, or did they put it in themselves?"

"Madame!" said Poirot, drawing himself up.

"I'm sorry, I'm sure, but you know what these papers are nowadays. You begin reading a nice article: 'What a bride said to her plain unmarried friend,' and it's all about a simple thing you buy at the chemist's and shampoo your hair with. Nothing but puff. But no offence taken, I hope? I'll tell you what I want you to do for me. I want you to find my cook."

Poirot stared at her; for once his ready tongue failed him. I turned aside to hide the broadening smile I could not control.

"It's all this wicked dole," continued the lady. "Putting ideas into servants' heads, wanting to be typists and what nots. Stop the dole, that's what I say. I'd like to know what *my* servants have to complain of—afternoon and evening off a week, alternate Sundays, washing put out, same food as we have—and never a bit of margarine in the house, nothing but the very best butter."

She paused for want of breath and Poirot seized his opportunity. He spoke in his haughtiest manner, rising to his feet as he did so.

"I fear you are making a mistake, madame. I am not holding an inquiry into the conditions of domestic service. I am a private detective."

"I know that," said our visitor. "Didn't I tell you I wanted you to find my cook for me? Walked out of the house on Wednesday, without so much as a word to me, and never came back."

"I am sorry, madame, but I do not touch this particular kind of business. I wish you good morning."

Our visitor snorted with indignation.

"That's it, is it, my fine fellow? Too proud, eh? Only deal with Government secrets and countesses' jewels? Let me tell you a servant's every bit as important as a tiara to a woman in my position. We can't all be fine ladies going out in our motors with our diamonds and our pearls. A good cook's a good cook—and when you 'lose her, it's as much to you as her pearls are to some fine lady."

For a moment or two it appeared to be a toss up between Poirot's dignity and his sense of humour. Finally he laughed and sat down again.

"Madame, you are in the right, and I am in the wrong. Your remarks are just and intelligent. This case will be a novelty. Never yet have I hunted a missing domestic. Truly here is the problem of national importance that I was demanding of fate just before your arrival. *En avant*! You say this jewel of a cook went out on Wednesday and did not return. That is the day before yesterday."

"Yes, it was her day out."

"But probably, madame, she has met with

some accident. Have you inquired at any of the hospitals?"

"That's exactly what I thought yesterday, but this morning, if you please, she sent for her box. And not so much as a line to me! If I'd been at home, I'd not have let it go—treating me like that! But I'd just stepped out to the butcher."

"Will you describe her to me?"

"She was middle-aged, stout, black hair turning grey—most respectable. She'd been ten years in her last place. Eliza Dunn, her name was."

"And you had had—no disagreement with her on the Wednesday?"

"None whatsoever. That's what makes it all so queer."

"How many servants do you keep, madame?"

"Two. The house-parlourmaid, Annie, is a very nice girl. A bit forgetful and her head full of young men, but a good servant if you keep her up to her work."

"Did she and the cook get on well together?"

"They had their ups and downs, of course—but on the whole, very well."

"And the girl can throw no light on the mystery?"

"She says not—but you know what servants are—they all hang together."

"Well, well, we must look into this. Where did you say you resided, madame?"

"At Clapham; 88 Prince Albert Road."

"*Bien*, madame, I will wish you good morning,

and you may count upon seeing me at your residence during the course of the day."

Mrs. Todd, for such was our new friend's name, then took her departure. Poirot looked at me somewhat ruefully.

"Well, well, Hastings, this is a novel affair that we have here. The Disappearance of the Clapham Cook! Never, *never*, must our friend Inspector Japp get to hear of this!"

He then proceeded to heat an iron and carefully removed the grease spot from his grey suit by means of a piece of blotting paper. His moustaches he regretfully postponed to another day, and we set out for Clapham.

Prince Albert Road proved to be a street of small prim houses, all exactly alike, with neat lace curtains veiling the windows, and well-polished brass knockers on the doors.

We rang the bell at No. 88, and the door was opened by a neat maid with a pretty face. Mrs. Todd came out in the hall to greet us.

"Don't go, Annie," she cried. "This gentleman's a detective and he'll want to ask you some questions."

Annie's face displayed a struggle between alarm and a pleasurable excitement.

"I thank you, madame," said Poirot bowing. "I would like to question your maid now—and to see her alone, if I may."

We were shown into a small drawing room, and

when Mrs. Todd, with obvious reluctance, had left the room, Poirot commenced his cross-examination.

"*Voyons, Mademoiselle Annie,* all that you shall tell us will be of the greatest importance. You alone can shed any light on the case. Without your assistance I can do nothing."

The alarm vanished from the girl's face and the pleasurable excitement became more strongly marked.

"I'm sure, sir," she said, "I'll tell you anything I can."

"That is good." Poirot beamed approval on her. "Now, first of all what is your own idea? You are a girl of remarkable intelligence. That can be seen at once! What is your own explanation of Eliza's disappearance?"

Thus encouraged, Annie fairly flowed into excited speech.

"White slavers, sir, I've said so all along! Cook was always warning me against them. 'Don't you sniff no scent, or eat any sweets—no matter how gentlemanly the fellow!' Those were her words to me. And now they've got her! I'm sure of it. As likely as not, she's been shipped to Turkey or one of them Eastern places where I've heard they like them fat!"

Poirot preserved an admirable gravity.

"But in that case—and it is indeed an idea!— would she have sent for her trunk?"

"Well, I don't know, sir. She'd want her things—even in those foreign places."

"Who came for the trunk—a man?"

"It was Carter Paterson, sir."

"Did you pack it?"

"No, sir, it was already packed and corded."

"Ah! That's interesting. That shows that when she left the house on Wednesday, she had already determined not to return. You see that, do you not?"

"Yes, sir." Annie looked slightly taken aback. "I hadn't thought of that. But it might still have been white slavers, mightn't it, sir?" she added wistfully.

"Undoubtedly!" said Poirot gravely. He went on: "Did you both occupy the same bedroom?"

"No, sir, we had separate rooms."

"And had Eliza expressed any dissatisfaction with her present post to you at all? Were you both happy here?"

"She'd never mentioned leaving. The place is all right—" The girl hesitated.

"Speak freely," said Poirot kindly. "I shall not tell your mistress."

"Well, of course, sir, she's a caution, Missus is. But the food's good. Plenty of it, and no stinting. Something hot for supper, good outings, and as much frying-fat as you like. And anyway, if Eliza did want to make a change, she'd never have gone off this way, I'm sure. She'd have stayed her month. Why, Missus could have a month's wages out of her for doing this!"

"And the work, it is not too hard?"

"Well, she's particular—always poking round in corners and looking for dust. And then there's the lodger, or paying guest as he's always called. But that's only breakfast and dinner, same as Master. They're out all day in the City."

"You like your master?"

"He's all right—very quiet and a bit on the stingy side."

"You can't remember, I suppose, the last thing Eliza said before she went out?"

"Yes, I can. 'If there's any stewed peaches over from the dining room,' she says, 'we'll have them for supper, and a bit of bacon and some fried potatoes.' Mad over stewed peaches, she was. I shouldn't wonder if they didn't get her that way."

"Was Wednesday her regular day out?"

"Yes, she had Wednesdays and I had Thursdays."

Poirot asked a few more questions, then declared himself satisfied. Annie departed, and Mrs. Todd hurried in, her face alight with curiosity. She had, I felt certain, bitterly resented her exclusion from the room during our conversation with Annie. Poirot, however, was careful to soothe her feelings tactfully.

"It is difficult," he explained, "for a woman of exceptional intelligence such as yourself, madame, to bear patiently the roundabout methods we poor detectives are forced to use. To have patience with stupidity is difficult for the quick-witted."

Having thus charmed away any little resentment on Mrs. Todd's part, he brought the conversation round to her husband and elicited the information that he worked with a firm in the City and would not be home until after six.

"Doubtless he is very disturbed and worried by this unaccountable business, eh? It is not so?"

"He's never worried," declared Mrs. Todd. " 'Well, well, get another, my dear.' That's all *he* said! He's so calm that it drives me to distraction sometimes. 'An ungrateful woman,' he said. 'We are well rid of her.' "

"What about the other inmates of the house, madame?"

"You mean Mr. Simpson, our paying guest? Well, as long as he gets his breakfast and his evening meal all right, *he* doesn't worry."

"What is his profession, madame?"

"He works in a bank." She mentioned its name, and I started slightly, remembering my perusal of the *Daily Blare*.

"A young man?"

"Twenty-eight, I believe. Nice quiet young fellow."

"I should like to have a few words with him, and also with your husband, if I may. I will return for that purpose this evening. I venture to suggest that you should repose yourself a little, madame, you look fatigued."

"I should just think I am! First the worry about Eliza, and then I was at the sales practically all yesterday, and you know what *that* is, M. Poirot, and what with one thing and another and a lot to do in the house, because of course Annie can't do it all—and very likely she'll give notice anyway, being unsettled in this way—well, what with it all, I'm tired out!"

Poirot murmured sympathetically, and we took our leave.

"It's a curious coincidence," I said, "but that absconding clerk, Davis, was from the same bank as Simpson. Can there be any connection, do you think?"

Poirot smiled.

"At the one end, a defaulting clerk, at the other a vanishing cook. It is hard to see any relation between the two, unless possibly Davis visited Simpson, fell in love with the cook, and persuaded her to accompany him on his flight!"

I laughed. But Poirot remained grave.

"He might have done worse," he said reprovingly. "Remember, Hastings, if you are going into exile, a good cook may be of more comfort than a pretty face!" He paused for a moment and then went on. "It is a curious case, full of contradictory features. I am interested—yes, I am distinctly interested."

II

That evening we returned to 88 Prince Albert Road and interviewed both Todd and Simpson. The former was a melancholy lantern-jawed man of forty-odd.

"Oh! Yes, yes," he said vaguely. "Eliza. Yes. A good cook, I believe. And economical. I make a strong point of economy."

"Can you imagine any reason for her leaving you so suddenly?"

"Oh, well," said Mr. Todd vaguely. "Servants, you know. My wife worries too much. Worn out from always worrying. The whole problem's quite simple really. 'Get another, my dear,' I say. 'Get another.' That's all there is to it. No good crying over spilt milk."

Mr. Simpson was equally unhelpful. He was a quiet inconspicuous young man with spectacles.

"I must have seen her, I suppose," he said. "Elderly woman, wasn't she? Of course, it's the other one I see always, Annie. Nice girl. Very obliging."

"Were those two on good terms with each other?"

Mr. Simpson said he couldn't say, he was sure. He supposed so.

"Well, we get nothing of interest there, *mon ami*," said Poirot as we left the house. Our departure had been delayed by a burst of vociferous repetition from Mrs. Todd, who repeated everything she had said that morning at rather greater length.

"Are you disappointed?" I asked. "Did you expect to hear something?"

Poirot shook his head.

"There was a possibility, of course," he said. "But I hardly thought it likely."

The next development was a letter which Poirot received on the following morning. He read it, turned purple with indignation, and handed it to me.

> Mrs. Todd regrets that after all she will not avail herself of Mr. Poirot's services. After talking the matter over with her husband she sees that it is foolish to call in a detective about a purely domestic affair. Mrs. Todd encloses a guinea for consultation fee.

III

"Aha!" cried Poirot angrily. "And they think to get rid of Hercule Poirot like that! As a favour—a great favour—I consent to investigate their miserable little twopenny-halfpenny affair—and they dismiss me *comme ça*! Here, I mistake not, is the hand of Mr. Todd. But I say no!—thirty-six times no! I will spend my own guineas, thirty-six hundred of them if need be, but I will get to the bottom of this matter!"

"Yes," I said. "But how?"

Poirot calmed down a little.

"*D'abord*," he said, "we will advertise in the papers. Let me see—yes—something like this: 'If Eliza Dunn will communicate with this address, she will hear of something to her advantage.' Put it in all the papers you can think of, Hastings. Then I will make some little inquiries of my own. Go, go—all must be done as quickly as possible!"

I did not see him again until the evening, when he condescended to tell me what he had been doing.

"I have made inquiries at the firm of Mr. Todd. He was not absent on Wednesday, and he bears a good character—so much for him. Then Simpson, on Thursday he was ill and did not come to the bank, but he was there on Wednesday. He was moderately friendly with Davis. Nothing out of the common. There does not seem to be anything there. No. We must place our reliance on the advertisement."

The advertisement duly appeared in all the principal daily papers. By Poirot's orders it was to be continued every day for a week. His eagerness over this uninteresting matter of a defaulting cook was extraordinary, but I realized that he considered it a point of honour to persevere until he finally succeeded. Several extremely interesting cases were brought to him about this time, but he declined them all. Every morning he would rush at his letters, scrutinize them earnestly and then lay them down with a sigh.

But our patience was rewarded at last. On the Wednesday following Mrs. Todd's visit, our landlady informed us that a person of the name of Eliza Dunn had called.

"*Enfin!*" cried Poirot. "But make her mount then! At once. Immediately."

Thus admonished, our landlady hurried out and returned a moment or two later, ushering in Miss Dunn. Our quarry was much as described: tall, stout, and eminently respectable.

"I came in answer to the advertisement," she explained. "I thought there must be some muddle or other, and that perhaps you didn't know I'd already got my legacy."

Poirot was studying her attentively. He drew forward a chair with a flourish.

"The truth of the matter is," he explained, "that your late mistress, Mrs. Todd, was much concerned about you. She feared some accident might have befallen you."

Eliza Dunn seemed very much surprised.

"Didn't she get my letter then?"

"She got no word of any kind." He paused, and then said persuasively: "Recount to me the whole story, will you not?"

Eliza Dunn needed no encouragement. She plunged at once into a lengthy narrative.

"I was just coming home on Wednesday night and had nearly got to the house, when a gentleman stopped me. A tall gentleman he was, with a beard and a big hat. 'Miss Eliza Dunn?' he said. 'Yes,' I said. 'I've been inquiring for you at No. 88,' he said. 'They told me I might meet you coming along here. Miss Dunn, I have come from Australia specially to find you. Do you happen to know the maiden name of your maternal grandmother?' 'Jane Emmott,' I said. 'Exactly,' he said. 'Now, Miss Dunn, although you may never have heard of the fact, your grandmother had a great friend, Eliza Leech. This friend went to Australia where she married a very wealthy settler. Her two children died in infancy, and she inherited all her husband's property. She died a few months ago, and by her will you inherit a house in this country and a considerable sum of money.'

"You could have knocked me down with a feather," continued Miss Dunn. "For a minute, I was suspicious, and he must have seen it, for he smiled. 'Quite right to be on your guard, Miss Dunn,' he said. 'Here are my credentials.' He handed me a letter from some lawyers in Melbourne, Hurst and Crotchet, and a card. He was Mr. Crotchet. 'There are one or two conditions,' he said. 'Our client was a little eccentric, you know. The bequest is conditional on your taking possession of the house (it is in Cumberland) before twelve o'clock tomorrow. The other condition is of no importance—it is merely a stipulation that you should not be in domestic service.' My face fell. 'Oh, Mr. Crotchet,' I said. 'I'm a cook. Didn't they tell you at the house?' 'Dear, dear,' he said. 'I had no idea of such a thing. I thought you might possibly be a companion or governess there. This is very unfortunate—very unfortunate indeed.'

" 'Shall I have to lose all the money?' I said, anxious like. He thought for a minute or two. 'There are always ways of getting round the law, Miss Dunn,' he said at last. 'We as lawyers know that. The way out here is for you to have left your employment this afternoon.' 'But my month?' I said. 'My dear Miss Dunn,' he said with a smile. 'You can leave an employer any minute by forfeiting a month's wages. Your mistress will understand in view of the circumstances. The difficulty is *time!* It is imperative that you should catch the 11.05 from King's Cross to the north. I can advance you ten pounds or so for the fare, and you can write a note at the station to your employer. I will take it to her myself and explain the whole circumstances.' I agreed, of course, and an hour later I was in the train, so flustered that I didn't know whether I was on my head or heels. Indeed by the time I got to Carlisle, I was half inclined to think the whole thing was one of those confidence tricks you read about. But I went to the address he had given me—solicitors they were, and it was all right. A nice little house, and an income of three hundred a year. These lawyers knew very little, they'd just got a letter from a gentleman in London instructing them to hand over the house to me and £150 for the first six months. Mr. Crotchet sent up my things to me, but there was no word from Missus. I supposed she was angry and grudged me my bit of luck. She kept back my box too, and sent my clothes in paper parcels. But there, of course if she never had my letter, she might think it a bit cool of me."

Poirot had listened attentively to this long history. Now he nodded his head as though completely satisfied.

"Thank you, mademoiselle. There had been, as you say, a little muddle. Permit me to recompense you for your trouble." He handed her an envelope. "You return to Cumberland immediately? A little word in your ear. *Do not forget how to cook.* It is always useful to have something to fall back upon in case things go wrong."

"Credulous," he murmured, as our visitor departed, "but perhaps not more than most of her class." His face grew grave. "Come, Hastings, there is no time to be lost. Get a taxi while I write a note to Japp."

Poirot was waiting on the doorstep when I returned with the taxi.

"Where are we going?" I asked anxiously.

"First, to despatch this note by special messenger."

This was done, and reentering the taxi Poirot gave the address to the driver.

"Eighty-eight Prince Albert Road, Clapham."

"So we are going there?"

"*Mais oui*. Though frankly I fear we shall be too late. Our bird will have flown, Hastings."

"Who is our bird?"

Poirot smiled.

"The inconspicuous Mr. Simpson."

"What?" I exclaimed.

"Oh, come now, Hastings, do not tell me that all is not clear to you now!"

"The cook was got out of the way, I realize that," I said, slightly piqued. "But why? *Why* should Simpson wish to get her out of the house? Did she know something about him?"

"Nothing whatever."

"Well, then—"

"But he wanted something that she had."

"Money? The Australian legacy?"

"No, my friend—something quite different." He paused a moment and then said gravely: "*A battered tin trunk....*"

I looked sideways at him. His statement seemed so fantastic that I suspected him of pulling my leg, but he was perfectly grave and serious.

"Surely he could buy a trunk if he wanted one," I cried.

"He did not want a new trunk. He wanted a trunk of pedigree. A trunk of assured respectability."

"Look here, Poirot," I cried, "this really is a bit thick. You're pulling my leg."

He looked at me.

"You lack the brains and the imagination of Mr. Simpson, Hastings. See here: On Wednesday evening, Simpson decoys away the cook. A printed card and a printed sheet of notepaper are simple matters to obtain, and he is willing to pay £150 and a year's house rent to assure the success of his plan. Miss Dunn does not recognize him— the beard and the hat and the slight colonial accent completely deceive her. That is the end of Wednesday—except for the trifling fact that Simpson has helped himself to fifty thousand pounds' worth of negotiable securities."

"*Simpson*—but it was *Davis*—"

"If you will kindly permit me to continue, Hastings! Simpson knows that the theft will be discovered on Thursday afternoon. He does not go to the bank on Thursday, but he lies in wait for Davis when he comes out to lunch. Perhaps he admits the theft and tells Davis he will return the securities to him—anyhow he succeeds in getting Davis to come to Clapham with him. It is the maid's day out, and Mrs. Todd was at the sales, so there is no one in the house. When the theft is discovered and Davis is missing, the implication will be overwhelming. Davis is the thief! Mr. Simpson will be perfectly safe, and can return to work on the morrow like the honest clerk they think him."

"And Davis?"

Poirot made an expressive gesture, and slowly shook his head.

"It seems too cold-blooded to be believed, and yet what other explanation can there be, *mon ami*. The one difficulty for a murderer is the disposal of the body—and Simpson had planned that out beforehand. I was struck at once by the fact that although Eliza Dunn obviously meant to return that night when she went out (witness her remark about the stewed peaches) *yet her trunk was all ready packed when they came for it*. It was Simpson who sent word to Carter Paterson to call on Friday and it was Simpson who corded up the box on Thursday afternoon. What suspicion could possibly arise? A maid leaves and sends for her box, it is labelled and addressed ready in her name, probably to a railway station within easy reach of London. On Saturday afternoon, Simpson, in his Australian disguise, claims it, he affixes a new label and address and redespatches it somewhere else, again 'to be left till called for.' When the authorities get suspicious, for excellent reasons, and open it, all that can be elicited will be that a bearded colonial despatched it from some junction near London. There will be nothing to connect it with 88 Prince Albert Road. Ah! Here we are."

Poirot's prognostications had been correct. Simpson had left days previously. But he was not to escape the consequences of his crime. By the aid of wireless, he was discovered on the *Olympia*, en route to America.

A tin trunk, addressed to Mr. Henry Wintergreen, attracted the attention of railway officials at Glasgow. It was opened and found to contain the body of the unfortunate Davis.

Mrs. Todd's cheque for a guinea was never cashed. Instead Poirot had it framed and hung on the wall of our sitting room.

"It is to me a little reminder, Hastings. Never to despise the trivial—the undignified. A disappearing domestic at one end—a cold-blooded murder at the other. To me, one of the most interesting of my cases."

About the Author

Agatha Christie is the most widely published author of all time and in any language, outsold only by the Bible and Shakespeare. Her books have sold more than a billion copies in English and another billion in a hundred foreign languages. She is the author of eighty crime novels and short-story collections, nineteen plays, two memoirs, and six novels written under the name Mary Westmacott.

She first tried her hand at detective fiction while working in a hospital dispensary during World War I, creating the now legendary Hercule Poirot with her debut novel *The Mysterious Affair at Styles*. With *The Murder at the Vicarage*, published in 1930, she introduced another beloved sleuth, Miss Jane Marple. Additional series characters include the husband-and-wife crime-fighting team of Tommy and Tuppence Beresford, private investigator Parker Pyne, and Scotland Yard detectives Superintendent Battle and Inspector Japp.

Many of Christie's novels and short stories were adapted into plays, films, and television series. *The Mousetrap*, her most famous play of all, opened in 1952 and is the longest-running play in history. Among her best-known film adaptations are *Murder on the Orient Express* (1974) and *Death on the Nile* (1978), with Albert Finney and Peter Ustinov playing Hercule Poirot, respectively. On the small screen Poirot has been most memorably portrayed by David Suchet, and Miss Marple by Joan Hickson and subsequently Geraldine McEwan and Julia McKenzie.

Christie was first married to Archibald Christie and then to archaeologist Sir Max Mallowan, whom she accompanied on expeditions to countries that would also serve as the settings for many of her novels. In 1971 she achieved one of Britain's highest honors when she was made a Dame of the British Empire. She died in 1976 at the age of eighty-five. Her one hundred and twentieth anniversary was celebrated around the world in 2010.

www.AgathaChristie.com

Also by Agatha Christie and available from
Center Point Large Print:

Crooked House
They Came to Baghdad
Endless Night
Ordeal by Innocence
Towards Zero
Death Comes as the End
The Pale Horse
Destination Unknown
Parker Pyne Investigates
The Secret of Chimneys
The Seven Dials Mystery
The Sittaford Mystery
Why Didn't They Ask Evans?
The Mysterious Mr. Quin
Sparkling Cyanide
The Harlequin Tea Set and Other Stories
The Man in the Brown Suit
Double Sin and Other Stories
Three Blind Mice and Other Stories
The Regatta Mystery and Other Stories
*The Witness for the Prosecution
   and Other Stories*
Murder Is Easy
Passenger to Frankfurt

Hercule Poirot Mystery Series:

The Murder of Roger Ackroyd
Death on the Nile
The A.B.C. Murders
Five Little Pigs
The Big Four
Poirot Investigates
Dead Man's Folly
One, Two, Buckle My Shoe
Murder in Mesopotamia
Lord Edgware Dies
Taken at the Flood
The Murder on the Links
The Hollow
Hallowe'en Party
After the Funeral
Cards on the Table
Cat Among the Pigeons
Death in the Clouds
Dumb Witness
The Clocks
Third Girl
Three Act Tragedy
Sad Cypress
Appointment with Death
Evil Under the Sun
Hickory Dickory Dock
The Mysterious Affair at Styles
The Mystery of the Blue Train
Peril at End House
Murder in the Mews
Hercule Poirot's Christmas
The Labors of Hercules

Miss Marple Mystery Series:
The Murder at the Vicarage
The Body in the Library
The Moving Finger
A Murder Is Announced
They Do It with Mirrors
4:50 from Paddington
A Caribbean Mystery
A Pocket Full of Rye
At Bertram's Hotel
Nemesis
Miss Marple: The Complete Short Stories
The Mirror Crack'd from Side to Side

Tommy and Tuppence Mystery Series:
The Secret Adversary
N or M?
By the Pricking of My Thumbs
Partners in Crime
Postern of Fate

Center Point Large Print
600 Brooks Road / PO Box 1
Thorndike ME 04986-0001 USA

(207) 568-3717

US & Canada:
1 800 929-9108
www.centerpointlargeprint.com